DETERMINISM

a Life. Destiny. Fate. *novel*

The story of Cara and Abel.

LK COLLINS

ISBN: 978-0-578-13401-7

Table of Contents

Dedication

To my forever friend, Miranda, this book would not be what it is without you. You're one in a million, babe. Don't ever forget that.

Prologue

-ABEL-

As I pull my Harley in the underground parking garage of my building, I cut the engine just as my cell phone rings. Still straddling my bike, I pull it out of my back pocket to see it's my brother calling.

I hit the answer button. "What's up, bro?"

"Hey, not much. How are you?"

"Dude, I'm fucking beat. We trained all week in a building that was hot as hell, and I carried more hose on my back than I knew was possible."

"Well, you are the new fire chief, so you gotta show those guys how to get shit done."

I laugh, "I guess. Anyways, what's up?"

"I'm sorry, I know this is last minute, but I told Lex that I invited you to the movies with us tonight, so she invited her friend, Cara. I don't want to look like an ass because I forgot to call you earlier. So, can you meet us there in an hour?"

Fuck, I hate the movies. I'm not a fan of crowds and this is the last thing I want to do tonight. But for my brother, I'll do anything. "Is Cara hot?"

"Yeah."

"Fine, text me where to meet you guys and I'll be there. She better be fucking smoking for me to see a movie at the theater."

"Don't worry, she is," he says and hangs up.

I get off my bike and walk to the elevator. I can't wait to get into the hot shower. My body is exhausted; every one of my muscles feels tense from work. I wish I could just chill tonight. But who knows? Maybe it won't be a waste, and I'll end up banging this chick. It's been weeks since I've gotten laid and I'm tired of the same bar flies that always flock to me because of my tattoos.

The elevator finally arrives and I press the button for the eighteenth floor. Living in the heart of downtown affords me a killer view. I just moved into this place and it's insane. Entering my spacious loft, the sun is bright and shining in all of the windows. Puss, my needy ass cat, runs up to me and winds in and out of my legs. She's a vocal, little bitch, but the only one I want.

I set my helmet on the counter, along with my keys, and grab a beer from the fridge. Cracking it open, I walk to the expansive wall of windows that is the back of my loft. I look out onto the city and take a pull of my beer.

Fuck, I'm tired.

Heading into the bathroom, I turn the shower on

and strip out of my clothes. As much as I love being a firefighter, the stench from the smoke is brutal. I take my time washing to ensure I'm clean. It's crazy how the faintest scent will drive you nuts. But who am I to complain? I'm doing my dream job and loving it. I've always had a passion for helping others. Plus the pay is awesome — fighting wildfires for twenty hours straight for a few months in the summer pays my bills for a year.

Stepping out of the shower, I wrap a towel around my waist and grab my toothbrush. My phone chimes while I brush my teeth. I walk back into the kitchen and grab it. It's Vincent, and of course we are meeting at a theater way across town. I dress quickly in jeans and a t-shirt, and grab a hat on my way out the door. I take my truck instead of my bike. The adrenaline rush I get from my bike can be a lot to handle, and I don't need any of that tonight.

I pull up to the theater right on time and park far away like I always do, taking my time as I walk up to the building. I approach and there are lots of people all around. I look for Alexa and Vincent, but don't spot them.

I lean up against the hard, brick wall and put my hands in my pockets. Looking down, I kick the loose gravel with my boots. Just two hours, and then I'll be home. If I weren't so tired it wouldn't be so bad. I check my phone noticing that those fuckers are late. I hate it when people aren't on time; I sure as hell can't show up late to a fire. Why does everyone else not give a shit about running on time?

When I take my eyes off of the ground, I look up and am immediately connected to a cute blonde. I watch her as she gets out of an Audi A4. Her red flats hit the pavement, and she slings a huge purse over her shoulder. She walks and I swear she is heading right towards me. I get a sense of déjà vu, like I've seen her before. My eyes scan down her perfectly built body — man, she's ridiculous. Her boobs are about to pop out of the top of her dress and those long, tan legs make my dick stir. *Fuck.*

My daydream is interrupted by my brother and Alexa as they approach her. Alexa hugs her and they continue towards me. Shit, this is the girl Vincent was telling me about. I fidget with the bill of my hat and then push myself off the wall.

"Come on, you know how cold theaters get, and you're barely wearing any clothes," Alexa says.

That's right, she is barely wearing any clothes, and I want to see her in even less. "I'll keep her warm," I say and can't help the smirk that's on my face.

She laughs at me. *Ouch.*

"I'll be just fine, thank you very much," she says in a mocking tone.

What the hell? I try again, giving her my best smile. "Are you sure? I'm happy to do the job."

She rolls her eyes at me and Vincent interjects. "All right, guys, let's not start the night off fighting. Cara, this is my brother, Abel. Abel, this is Cara, Alexa's best friend."

Suddenly I feel nervous reaching for her hand to kiss the top of it; this has to get her to warm up to me and stop being so cold. "It's a pleasure to meet you, Cara." I say and notice a small tattoo on the inside of her wrist. That's where I know her from — she's a nurse at University Hospital. I knew I had seen her before. I rode in with a patient once during transport while providing care. How could I forget her — not to mention how gorgeous she is — and those eyes? Yeah, this is definitely her. She has the most alluring aqua-colored eyes I've ever seen.

She pulls her hand back and wipes it on my shoulder. Everyone laughs at her gesture, and we head inside the theater. I tag along still in a fog; I could never forget the color of her eyes.

~ *Cara* ~

Why will my hair never cooperate? Not that it matters, but still, I don't want to look like garbage. I try again to pull my brush through my thick blond hair. I look over my shoulder at the clock on my nightstand. *Damn it.* I'm running late — again. I finish ripping the brush through my tangled strands. God, it needs a cut; it's almost to my ass. I slide on my red, patent leather flats and leave my room.

I have ten minutes to make it to the theater to meet my best friend, Alexa, and her new boyfriend, Vincent. Alexa said Vincent's brother is going to be there. She also told me he's covered in tattoos, which is my typical MO, but I've turned over a new leaf. I know it's going to be hard to resist, but that was the old Cara. The new Cara has sworn off tattooed bad boys.

Sliding behind the wheel of my Audi A4, I toss my purse on the passenger seat and fly out of the neighborhood. Of course traffic sucks; it's always bad in Denver this time of day. I roll along, wishing I could go faster, but I can't. You know what, who cares? It's not like I care what this guy thinks, and Alexa is always late.

I pull up to the theater and it takes forever to find a parking spot close to the entrance. Once I do, I'm out and heading towards the front. I look for Alexa and Vincent, but don't see them. Ahh, there they are.

"Hey, girl. You look cute. I hope you brought a sweater," Alexa says.

"Thanks, and no, I didn't. Why would I need a sweater in August?"

"Come on, you know how cold theaters get, and you're barely wearing any clothes."

Before I can answer I look up and see a tattooed god. *Shit.* Is that Vincent's brother? As we walk towards him, his eyes are glued to mine, and my heart starts to race. His hat is low, just how I like. He has his hands tucked into his pockets, making his forearms flex and his tattoos that much more visible. I look away from his hazel eyes. *Pull your shit together, Cara. You're done with guys like this.*

"I'll keep her warm," he says.

The hell you will.

It's time to be a bitch. I laugh at him, "I'll be just fine, thank you very much."

"Are you sure? I'm happy to do the job," he says looking deep into my eyes. His intensity makes me instantly wet between my legs. It takes all of my willpower to not play right into his game. Then he grabs my hand and kisses the top of it. My body tingles from his touch, and instantly I want more.

Fuck. I need more.

As I snap out of it, I pull my hand away from his and wipe it on his shoulder. I will *not* be hurt by another asshole with tattoos. Quickly I walk ahead of him and latch onto Alexa, leaving Abel behind and pushing away the emotions he has coursing through my body.

Chapter 1

Hi

I hit the pavement hard, running in my Nikes. I push myself to try and clear my head as the music blasts through my earbuds. These last eight months have been frustrating to say the least. I've made it my mission to avoid Abel, but for some reason, everywhere I turn … there he is. He is determined to win me over by any means necessary, and I'm not going to give in. I'm focusing on myself, plain and simple. Or at least that's what I keep saying to convince my own mind that he's out to hurt me, like all the douchebags from my past. I've tried to be a bitch, but it just makes him push that much more. His determination drives me mad with sexual energy. He does things to me; my body reacts to his intensity and grit like nothing I've ever known. He makes my heart pound and I instantly lose focus. All I can think about are his hands on my body … and that mouth.

I come up to a streetlight and have to stop. I lean

over to catch my breath, resting my hands on my knees, breathing in rigidly until the light changes, and then I mentally whip myself to keep going. I feel winded, but it doesn't matter. I can't clear my head. By the time my iPod stops the playlist I set it on, I look down and realize I've been running for over an hour. Turning around, I head back and keep a steady pace. Feeling parched from being unprepared and bolting out of the house without a water bottle, I spot a smoothie shop and head towards it.

When I walk in, there's a small line but it allows me to mull over the menu. I decide on my order right as I'm called. While I wait for my drink, I look out at the beautiful Cherry Creek District that is my home. The snow has all melted and spring is in full effect. The trees are blooming and the grass is almost green. The door chimes open and I look to see a guy I recognize from the hospital come in. He looks right at me and smiles. If I remember correctly, I think he works in Radiation.

"Cara, is that you?" he asks.

"Yup. It's Ben, right?"

"Yeah. What are you doing here?" he asks tilting his head to the side.

"I'm on my way home from a run and thought I would grab a smoothie. What about you?"

"I just got done with a yoga class. I usually come here afterwards."

They call my drink and he grabs it, handing it to me with the straw.

9

I smile at him. "Thanks. Are you going to order?"

He bobs his head and we get in line together. Ben is a little taller than me, probably five ten. His hair is blonde and his eyes are blue. He's not the kind of guy I would typically be interested in, but this is the new Cara, so I force myself to see if there's any chemistry. I *need* to let go of all thoughts of Abel.

Ben orders and once his drink is ready he asks, "Do you want to sit outside?"

"Sure," I say. Following him as he opens the door for me, we find a tiny table in the sun.

"So, Cara, tell me about yourself," he says with a straight expression on his face. He is completely open about wanting to get to know me. I shrug my shoulders not sure where to start. He laughs at me. "Okay, I'll start then. I'll tell you one thing about me and you have to tell me the same thing about yourself." I nod my head, liking this game already. It makes him have to come up with the questions.

"My favorite food is Italian."

"My favorite food is anything seafood."

He cocks an eyebrow at me, "See? That wasn't so hard."

I laugh and take a sip of my smoothie.

"I have a dog."

"I don't have any pets."

"I'm single."

"I'm single too."

10

He smiles, "I work today."

"I work today too."

"Will you have lunch with me then?" he asks.

I smile and nod my head, unsure of how to respond to his brazenness.

"Good, I'll swing by and grab you." He looks down at his watch, "I gotta run. I have another yoga class to teach." He gets up and pulls his sunglasses down over his eyes. "I'll see you later."

"Bye."

He turns around and walks off, his shorts hugging his ass in just the right way. While I watch him, I wonder, could I be attracted to someone like him? He seems genuine and has a fun personality. I guess at lunch I'll find out more. If anything he will help keep my mind off Abel and stick to the new Cara.

I finish my smoothie and throw the cup away. Then I sprint home, shower, and head to work. I hate working swing shifts, and I've had to work a lot of them lately. As soon as I get to work and head to check on my first patient, I hear my name called over the intercom.

"Cara Savannah to reception, Cara Savannah to reception." Damn it, I bet there's another walk-in to the ER demanding that I have them seen quicker than the two-hour wait they've been quoted. I place the clipboard on the slot of Mr. Parson's door and head out.

"Hey, Margaret, you paged me?"

"Yes, dear, you have a visitor."

I give her a surprised look. Who would be visiting me here at work? She points into the waiting area of the ER, and leaning up against the wall is Abel. As soon as I look at him, he smirks at me, and I swallow hard. *What is he doing here?* He's clearly working, dressed in his Denver Fire gear. I exit and head towards him, a mixture of butterflies and sexual frenzy flowing through my system. I mask that by putting on my angry face.

"What are you doing here?" I snap.

"Well, hello to you as well," he says giving me that panty-dropping smile and continues, "We're doing our monthly inspection and I thought I would say hi."

I cross my arms over my chest in my pink scrubs, pretending to have a dislike for him, when really I want exactly what he is pushing for. "Hi," I sarcastically quip back.

"Really, you're going to act like that?"

"Like what? You came to say hi, so I returned the gesture. Do you need anything else?"

Clearly I've frustrated him, because he runs his hands over his face and his brown hair. Looking back into my eyes, he grabs my arm and drags me outside. I follow along, enjoying his touch way too much to try and pull away. Once we are outside and alone, he locks his eyes with mine. He is inches from my face and I can feel his hot breath on my skin. He smells fucking delicious, making my entire body tingle.

"Cara, have I done something to upset you?" he demands.

I shake my head.

"Then what's your problem? Obviously there is something going on between us and you've been fighting it for months."

"I don't have a problem. I'm just surprised to see you here. And for the record, I'm not interested in dating anyone."

"Good, neither am I."

An awkward silence takes over and all I can focus on is the sound of our breathing. It's harsh and ragged. He still has a tight grip on my arm, and his hand is hot. I imagine what it would feel like on the rest of my body. He leans into my neck and I clamp my eyes shut. He doesn't move as his breath continues to wash over my skin. He takes his right arm and slides it behind me, pulling me tightly against him. Instinctively I lean my head to the side and wait for his lips to drench my skin. A loud horn goes off causing me to jump. Abel barely moves and when I look at him, he is looking into my eyes.

I look behind him and a huge fire truck is parked in front of the ER entrance. I feel his grip on me loosen as our eyes reconnect.

"This isn't finished," he says.

But it is. It has to be. I promised myself not to get involved with someone like him. Call me a bitch, or whatever you want, but I've had my heart smashed way too many times by guys just like this. I've never been in an honest and trusting relationship and I want that. I know with Abel, it's not possible. Not with what I've heard about his womanizing track record from Lex. I've lasted eight months fighting this, and I'm not about to give in now.

"Yes. It is," I whisper.

I turn and walk away from what feels so right, but I *know* deep down is wrong. For the remainder of the day, I dive into my work and keep busy concentrating on my patients. There's a reason I'm a nurse — it's internally healing and therapeutic to have an impact on other people's lives. I keep that as my focus until I turn around and see that sitting on my desk at the nurses' station is a yellow rose. There's a note beneath it with my name written in cursive.

Meet me on the roof at 6:00pm for our lunch-dinner. ☺Ben

Ahh, what a sweet guy. I check my watch and it's a quarter till six. I find Elaina, my boss, and clear my lunchtime with her. I have butterflies in my stomach because of the excitement. I know that it's only fifteen minutes, but I just might keel over in anticipation. Trying to keep busy, I pace the floor and make sure all of my patients are okay, the minutes feeling like hours, and finally I look at the clock and see it's 5:59. I bolt, waving bye to Elaina as I pass her office. On the elevator ride up, each floor ticks by and I know time is dragging only because I *love* surprises. I mean, I really, *really* love them.

Once the doors finally open, I exit and walk down the white hallway that leads to the roof. My palms are sweaty as I reach for the door handle. I open it and Ben is up here, sitting with his back to me at the edge of the roof. When the door clicks shut, he turns towards me. Getting up with a huge smile on his face he walks to me. "You made it," he says giving me a hug.

"Of course I did. Were you having doubts?"

He rubs the back of his head, "Nah."

Bullshit.

But I'm not about to call him out on it. I don't know him well enough. "Come on. The sun's about to set," he says walking to the edge where he has a blanket laid out and two boxed lunches.

"This is really sweet of you. Thank you," I say.

"No problem. I did what I could considering we are both working. So take your pick, tuna or turkey."

"You know I love seafood. I'll take the tuna."

"That's why I got it."

As we sit, I wonder why I've never come up here myself. Sitting down, my feet dangle over the edge and my stomach tightens with excitement as I stare at the ground. I love heights and anything that sparks an adrenaline rush. Taking my eyes off of the ground, I pull them up to the sky and I'm stunned by the sight in front of me. The sky is a mixture of pinks and blues.

"Damn, it's gorgeous."

"It is. Do you ever come up here?" he asks.

"No, I don't."

"Really? Why not?"

I can't help but giggle. "I was just wondering the same thing. I guess I've never thought of it. In the ER, I'm so busy, when I take a break I grab some food and head back."

"Cara, you have to step away from work and enjoy things like this or else you're going to get burned out. I can see the passion you have for your work and your patients. I've noticed it for quite some time. Don't let that fizzle away because you aren't taking time for yourself."

"I'll do my best to remember that."

"Let's eat and then you can tell me why on earth you're single."

I laugh again at his boldness. He really just speaks his mind. Like earlier at the smoothie shop when we sat down and he blurted out "Tell me about yourself." At that point, I didn't even know a thing about him, minus that we worked together.

I unwrap my tuna sandwich and take a bite, looking again at the sky. It's now a mixture of pinks and purples.

"Are you going to tell me?" he asks.

I swallow and look at his blue eyes and messy hair. "Why don't you tell me first?"

"You do that a lot, don't you?"

"What?" I ask, confused.

"Switch the conversation off of yourself."

"No, I don't," I argue back.

"Well, you've done it twice with me."

I take a long sigh and realize maybe I have been avoiding certain questions. "I've never had luck in the dating department. I always fall for the wrong guys and end up getting my heart hurt. I'm tired of doing the same thing and expecting different results, so I'm taking a new approach and letting love take a back seat so I can change my ways."

He swallows a bite of his sandwich and asks, "So why are you on a date with me?"

"Because you're different than the guys I typically fall for. Plus, my lunch date today cancelled," I joke and nudge his shoulder with mine in hopes he will drop this topic. We're both silent as we eat. Ben doesn't bring up my reasons for not dating or why I'm single again and for that I'm grateful.

"Thank you for this," I say.

"It was my pleasure," he says and looks deep into my eyes. Searching his, I look for an attraction. I want to be drawn to him. However, there's something missing I just can't pinpoint.

Damn it, I'm doomed.

Chapter 2

Flatline

I pull up to the hospital for my last shift of the week and it looks like all hell is breaking loose. There are five ambulances and a few cop cars. I park and sprint to the first ambulance. Fuck, it's a kid. I hop in the back and take over squeezing the controlled ventilation bag from the EMT.

"What are his vitals?" I ask.

"BP is one-ten over sixty, and his pulse is strong. He was pulled out of a burning apartment building. He has no physical signs of injury. I believe at this point it's just smoke inhalation, but I don't know how long he's been unconscious for."

"Alright, let's get him inside and consult with an attending. We'll need to page the pediatric on-call doctor as well."

While we push the gurney inside, he suddenly goes into cardiac arrest. The EMT yells "code blue" and every available staff member comes over to help us. I watch in horror as this little guy quickly loses color, and I know we don't have much time.

"We need a crash cart," I yell.

Ron, the attending on duty, takes over while I cut open the boy's shirt and hook up the heart monitors. Jaime, another nurse, charges the paddles as I smear goo on his chest.

"CLEAR!" Ron shouts before sending a volt of electricity coursing through his body. We all put our hands in the air and step away from the patient. "Charging 200 joules," he says and shocks him, causing the boy to bow off of the bed. But we get nothing. The line on the monitor stays flat.

Ron shocks the boy again. The pediatric doctor arrives and assists. We all continue to work as a team on him for the next forty minutes, but never restart his heart. The time of death is called and that horrible sinking feeling comes over me. As much as I love my job, during times like this I absolutely loathe it. Losing a patient is never easy, but when it's a child, it's just heartbreaking.

I excuse myself and head outside. There's nothing else I can do. It was on my watch that someone's little boy died. Walking towards my car, I take a minute to myself on the way to grab my bag. Then I hear someone call my name. I turn to see Ben jogging towards me.

"Hey, are you okay?" he asks.

I shake my head not wanting to talk about what just happened. "Cara, talk to me. What's the matter?"

"I just lost a patient. A kid."

His expression changes to sorrow as he steps closer, wrapping me in his arms. I take comfort in his firm hold and tightly grip his t-shirt. The way he holds me is exactly what I need right now, and he doesn't push me to talk any further or ask more questions. We stand like this for a few minutes and when he pulls away from me, he rests his forehead on mine, and stares at me.

Looking into his eyes again like I did the other day, I don't feel anything and I pull away. "I have to get my bag out of my car."

He releases me. "Yeah, of course. Listen, I'm really sorry. Let me know if you need anything?"

I nod my head and when Ben turns to walk away from me, I see Abel standing at the entrance of the ER. Immediately I'm on pins and needles with anticipation as to why he is here. Abel turns away from me and walks inside. I continue to my car to grab my purse. I know I shouldn't be excited that Abel is here, but I can't help what I'm feeling. That spark that I'd hoped to feel with Ben ignites within me the moment I see Abel, even from a hundred feet away.

Walking back inside, I look for him but don't see him in the waiting room. I press the button on the wall allowing access to the ER and I see Abel at the end of the hallway.

Sonofabitch.

He's talking to Ben and is inches away from his face. Ben has his hands out to the sides of him and is shaking his head. I jog down the hall. "Abel, what the hell are you doing?"

He looks away from Ben and back to me. "I was just asking this little prick why he had his hands all over you in the parking lot."

"That's none of your business!"

Abel looks away from me and back to Ben. Clearly he is making this his business and doesn't give a damn how I feel.

Ben starts talking, "Cara just had a patient pass away and was upset. I was just trying to comfort her, that's all."

Abel's eyes are glued to mine. "I hope you're happy, Abel. And to make things clear, you don't have a right to care who the hell has their hands on me," I snap at him.

Ben walks away from us and I call after him. But he waves me off and disappears around the corner.

"Shit, I'm sorry. I had no idea," Abel says.

"Don't you think it's a little late for that? I mean, really. Who the hell do you think you are coming in here acting like this?"

He steps closer and I retreat a step. "Don't. I told you yesterday this was finished."

"I wasn't trying to do anything. I heard you. I'm sorry for how I just acted. You're right — it's not my place."

"Damn straight you have no right. You are so much to handle! What the hell are you doing here anyway?"

"One of my guys was brought in with smoke

inhalation so I came to check on him."

"Fine. What's his name and I'll take you to his room?"

"Troy Sorano."

"Okay, follow me." I turn and start walking, not waiting to see if he comes with me or not. But I can sense that he is behind me. How could you not sense someone with a presence like his? As we round the corner, I check the board and see that Troy is in room 114. Of course, I'm his nurse.

"Fuck, you stink," I quip at Abel.

"Sorry, I just left a fire. It was an apartment building, and pretty brutal."

I think back to the EMT telling me that the kid was pulled out of an apartment building. I wonder if Abel saved him. I turn to look at him as we approach Troy's room. He has his huge black and yellow firefighter pants on and a blue Denver Fire t-shirt. He has soot all over his arms and forehead. I realize now that I didn't even notice any of this when I first saw him. I open the door and we enter Troy's room.

"Hi Troy, I'm Cara. I found someone that came to see you." He opens his eyes to see Abel standing next to me and smiles.

"What's up, Chief? You didn't have to come here."

Abel smiles and sits in the chair next to his bed. "I know I didn't have to. I wanted to. Plus I'm supposed to be the last one out of any fire and your crazy ass didn't

22

listen to me when I said we needed to evacuate."

"I'm sorry, but there was a little boy in there and I couldn't leave him. I had to get him out."

"Don't be sorry. I'm just glad you're okay."

Troy looks over at me as I check his vitals and write them down on his chart. "Can you find out how that kid is doing?"

"Yeah," I say lying. I know in the pit of my stomach the kid who died is the one Troy pulled out. "I'm not sure if they brought him here, but I'll see what I can find out."

He smiles at me, and leans his head back into the pillow.

"You look beat, dude. I'm proud of you for today. I'll let you rest and stop by later to check on you." Abel says and pats his shoulder. As I exit the room, Abel is right behind me.

He grabs my arm and stops me before I go behind the nurses' station. Immediately his touch sparks my body, but this time I pull away. After seeing the way he reacted with Ben, I'm definitely not going to let myself get involved. I can see all of the characteristics in him that I'm desperate to avoid in a relationship. I need a man like Ben — sweet, thoughtful, and considerate. Not this brute who sweeps in like he has some caveman claim over me when I've made it clear I'm not his.

"Are you okay?" he asks.

I nod my head and rub my forehead feeling a headache come on.

"Listen, I'm sorry again for earlier," he says.

I put my hand up to stop him. "Walk with me?" I ask.

His eyes light up at my request and we leave the ER. We head outside, into another warm day, and I love the early summer weather. "I don't know how to tell Troy this, but I think the kid he pulled out of the fire earlier is the patient I lost."

"Oh shit, Cara, it was a kid?"

"Yeah. Why do you think I was so upset? I worked on him for forty fucking minutes, Abel."

He grabs me tightly and pulls me into his large body. I melt into him, unable to push him away. I can't fight what I know is wrong. Under the soot smell, I can still smell his scent that I love; it's so fresh that as I breathe in it tickles my nose. His chest is hard as a rock as he holds me. Tears gloss over my eyes and I don't know why — I never cry.

"Don't worry about Troy. I'll tell him, okay?"

I nod my head and I feel his lips press against my hair. Another ambulance pulls up and Jamie runs out of the ER. She looks over at us and yells to me, "Cara, I need you on this. I paged Ron, but it's just us for now."

Abel releases me and gently pushes me in the direction of the ambulance. I run towards the patient who is being pulled out of the back, although my body is screaming at me to stay put in his arms, where I feel safe and secure.

Chapter 3

Determination

I finally fall asleep after tossing and turning for hours. Just as I'm drifting off, my phone rings. "Noooooo," I say into my pillow and reach for my phone off of my nightstand.

"Hello," I croak without taking my face out of the pillow or looking at the screen.

"Cara?" a male voice asks.

"Yeah," I say and roll over.

"It's Vincent, are you okay?"

"I'm fine. I just woke up. What's up?"

"So you remember how you and I went ring shopping a few weeks ago. The jeweler called and the ring's ready. I want to ask Alexa to marry me today."

"Today as in this day?"

"Yeah. I'm not waiting any longer; I've waited long enough. Listen, I called because I need your help. I wanted to take her somewhere special and then she got this harebrained idea to have a BBQ since the weather is so nice. So I'm going to do it here. Do you think if I e-mailed you a list of what I need you could pick it all up and the ring too?"

"Of course."

"Thank God. I owe you. I don't have an excuse for sneaking away today, and I kind of already told the jeweler you would pick the ring up."

"You're really going to owe me," I joke.

"I know, thank you. I'll buy you anything you want."

"It's no problem. I'm glad you asked me and trust me to take care of it all."

We hang up and I stare at my screen. I scroll through my contacts and stumble upon Abel's name. I remember the night he programmed it in here. So many times I've been tempted to call him, just like I am now, but I haven't. Maybe I should change that. As my thumb hovers over the screen, an incoming call comes in from Alexa.

I answer it and drag my ass out of bed, "Hey, Lex."

"Morning, girl. I was thinking about having an impromptu BBQ today. Are you down?"

"Actually, I have plans," I say, completely joking.

"No. You have to come. Cancel your plans."

"I'm just messing with you. I'll be there. What time?"

"Four o'clock?"

"Sounds good. Text me if you need me to bring anything."

"You got it. I'll see you later."

I hang up and turn on the shower. I can't even imagine how excited Alexa is going to be tonight. I know she has dreamt of this happening, but always thought it was impossible. Finally today Vincent is going to make her dreams come true.

I get in the shower and wash myself, as well as my mane of hair. I'm thinking it's about time I get it cut. It's seriously down to my ass. I love to let it grow and then cut off twelve or so inches and donate it to Locks of Love for kids with alopecia.

I get out and dry off. As I do, I check my e-mail on my iPad and see Vincent has already sent over the list. God, that man is prepared. He needs white rose petals, preferably twenty dozen. *Holy hell.* White candles of different sizes and dimensions. And the ring.

I'm sure I'll have to go to at least ten different flower shops to get that many roses. I dress in a comfy, floor-length, cotton dress, grab my short jean jacket and put on a little makeup before I leave.

The errands weren't as bad as I thought they would be. I only had to go to six flower shops and two stores for the candles. I waited to grab the ring until last, since it costs more than a small house, and I didn't want it sitting in my car all day.

Pulling up to Alexa and Vincent's, I see Abel's truck

and a car I don't recognize. Shit, I should have figured he would be here. I sneak up to the door and peek inside, everyone is outback. *Hallelujah.* I run back to my car and grab the bags, then sneak inside. With the ring tucked safely in my purse, and my bags in hand I sprint across the great room and up the stairs.

Holy shitballs, talk about luck. I can't believe no one saw me and that damn dog didn't hear me come in. I bust open all the candles and begin to place them all over the room. Next I get to the rose petals, pulling the petals off all the roses and spreading them everywhere, practically carpeting the room and bed. Last but not least, I place the ring box in Vincent's nightstand.

Stepping back I take a look at my handiwork, I see I really have done an exceptional job. You would think he hired a professional to construct it all. Maybe I'm in the wrong career …

Heading downstairs, I hear Lex come in from the back patio. As I glance down the stairs, she is looking in the fridge and I quickly walk down and slide outside. When I pull the door shut, Abel looks at me and winks. I head straight to Vincent to fill him in on everything while she's inside.

"Hey, when did you get here?" Alexa asks me as she comes back out.

"I just got here. I snuck around back. I rang the doorbell, but no one answered."

"You could have just come in, Cara."

"It's fine really. Let me help you set this down so we can eat. I'm starving."

I take the food from her. The whole time Abel has had his eyes on me. I try to not focus on him or the fact he is watching my every move. We all sit to eat and I spark up conversation with Lincoln, Alexa's brother.

I can't help but picture him with my sister, Amber. He looks like just her type, and Lord knows she needs a sane, stable boyfriend in her life. Lincoln is funny and keeps me laughing, and I can tell Abel is annoyed. He hasn't touched his food and is sitting back just sipping on his beer. I need to get away from his glare, so I ask Alexa and Vincent, "Are you guys done?"

I collect their plates and head inside. When I reach for the sliding door, Abel opens it for me and my heart starts to pound.

Damn it, I was trying to take a minute away.

He follows me in and I place the plates in the sink. Leaning back on the opposite counter I brace myself. "Were you doing that on purpose?" he asks.

"Doing what?" I ask back, confused.

He steps closer to me and presses his pelvis against mine. Placing his hands on my hips, he stares into my eyes. "Flirting with Lincoln?"

I look back at him, letting him completely intoxicate me. "I wasn't flirting."

"Do you feel what you do to me? Do you have any idea the control you have over my body?"

I shake my head and close my eyes as he grinds his erection against my core. Fuck, it's been so long since I've been with anyone. This feels so good, quite possibly *too* good.

"Abel," his dad, Charlie, yells, causing him to pull away from me. I feel the blood rush to my face as my pussy throbs for more. Abel doesn't look back at me and walks away with his dad.

"Hey, girl," Jamie says as she bumps her butt with mine. We are standing at the quiet nurses' station and I'm wrapping up my paperwork before I head out. She is here for the night.

"What's up?"

"The girl in 115 is pretending to paint her nails, but she doesn't have nail polish. I think we need to get her a psych consult."

I laugh at her. "Really? Then order it."

"Will you sign off on it before you leave?"

I shake my head, "Nope. It has to be an attending or higher. I'm just a measly little nurse."

"You really should check her out before you go."

I grab my purse and sling it over my shoulder. "Nah. I'm sure she'll still be here tomorrow. Have a good night."

I walk out and head towards my car. It's warm tonight and I've got blood on my scrubs, so I take my scrub top off, wearing only a small, black cami and dig in my purse for my keys. When I look up, Abel is sitting next to my car. He is straddling his Harley and knows that I'm shocked. I can tell by the smug look on his face, as I stand there frozen searching for words.

"What's wrong, kitten? Cat got your tongue?"

"What the hell are you doing here?"

"I think the better question is what the hell are you doing? Why are you walking out of the hospital at almost midnight, not paying attention to your surroundings, and stripping off your clothes? You do realize that we don't work in the best part of town."

"Don't start with the protective shit again. I can do whatever I want, Abel."

"I know you can. That's why I want to ask you if you'll go on a ride with me tonight."

"It's almost midnight."

"I don't give a shit what time it is. Are there only certain times of day that you'll ride on a motorcycle?"

"No, but —"

"There will be no buts tonight, Cara, I can assure you of that. You've been through hell this week with work and losing a patient, and I'm sure you need to unwind. Just come on a ride with me."

"I've never ridden on a motorcycle before."

"It's okay. There's not much to know. I'll teach you

and I promise I'll be safe."

"Okay," I say way too excitedly. I can't believe he was sweet enough to think of me and come here. I wonder how long he waited for me to get off. I pop open my trunk and throw my purse in. Pulling out my hoodie I keep in case of emergencies or a breakdown. I slide it on, close my trunk, and zip my keys in the pocket.

I turn towards Abel and put my arms out to my sides. "Will this do?"

"Yup, you look perfect. Just put this on." He passes me a smooth, black helmet, and as I go to put it on, I notice there is still a tag on the inside.

"Can you take that out? It looks like it will hurt."

Laughing nervously, he takes the helmet from me, shredding the tag out of the inside and passes it back to me. "Here you go, sorry. I just bought it."

"It's alright," I say, throwing my leg over the bike.

"The best advice I can give you is to just relax. Let me control the bike. You don't weigh much so it shouldn't be a problem. Just keep close to me."

He starts the bike and it's an extremely loud rumble. It shakes my body, but after a few moments I get used to it. He pops the kickstand up and walks us backwards out of the parking spot. "You have to hold on, kitten." I wrap my arms around his leather-clad body, and he takes off, causing me to hold him tighter.

Excitement spikes through me as we move through the city. This is a pure adrenaline rush and I've never felt anything like this before. I rest my cheek against his shoulder and watch as everything passes us by. His scent is stronger now than ever before, and I wonder what it is that makes him smell so damn good. Each time we come to a stop he takes one of his hands and rests it on top of mine. Slowly stroking my skin or intertwining our fingers.

I don't want the ride to end, but I know I'm swimming in risky waters. As much as I want more with Abel, I know it will end in heartache, and I have to tell him that we have to just be friends. I enjoy being around him too much to risk ruining that. I also know the kind of person I am, and if I don't stop this now and things progress, then I will fall in love and that will scare him away. It's too hard to ignore him when we are around one another, so friends is going to have to work.

Slowly, he pulls back into the hospital parking lot. Once the bike stops, I hop off and remove my helmet, feeling a little unsteady from getting used to my own two feet again. He turns the bike off and looks at me confused. "Are you okay?"

"Yeah, I'm good. Thank you so much for taking me out. The ride was awesome, not to mention the rush. I don't know how you can ride this thing and stay calm."

He takes his helmet off as well. "It takes some getting used to, but you'll get there. So I did well for my first time having a passenger on the back of my bike?"

Say what?

There's no way I'm the only girl who has ever been

on the back of his bike. Then I remember the tag in the helmet and it clicks. *Holy shit, I am the only one!*

"Yeah, you did great," I reply, as I pop my trunk. I take my hoodie off and throw it in. I grab my purse and turn to look at Abel, but he is in a trance staring at my breasts. I look down and realize that my tank top is pulled really far down, almost exposing my firm nipples. Shit, I forgot a bra today too. Being sleep deprived must be affecting me.

I pull my tank top up. "Don't look at me like that. We're friends. Remember we agreed we didn't want to date anyone. You have to stop coming on to me like you've been. It's too risky for us to be anything more."

"I'm sorry, Cara, but I don't think I can just be your friend."

"Yes, you can," I demand, afraid to lose him. "Just try, okay?"

He nods his head and I walk over to him to give him a hug goodbye. I realize as I reach up, that my boobs are in his face and he is staring again. I slap him on the back of the head and walk off to my car. I turn back to him and he is rubbing his head watching my ass.

"Stop it," I yell. "You can't check out your friends."

He winks at me and I get into my car frustrated at how difficult he is making this.

Chapter 4

Date

The last few weeks have been boring. I've tried to talk to Ben, but every time I've gone to Radiation, he's been with a patient. Things have been quiet. I haven't heard much from anyone, except Alexa the night of the engagement when she called gushing. I couldn't be happier for her and I can't wait to get all of the details. She kept the conversation short as she said she had a million calls to make. Now I'm sitting on my couch enjoying my first day off in over a week, and am procrastinating doing anything productive. My eyes are heavy and I must have dozed off because my cell phone vibrates and makes me jump. I grab it off of my chest and look at the screen. It's a text from Abel. I haven't heard from him since our midnight ride, so I'm surprised that he texted me.

What are you wearing? Is he serious? That's the text he sends me after not talking to him for weeks? I text him back. **You can't ask your friends things like that. Oh** *wait. I haven't talked to you in so long, are we even still friends?*

There. That would sure piss him off. Is he crazy? Well, I guess I am talking about Abel and he's definitely a bit out there. *Sorry, wrong person. I didn't mean to send that to you. You know this friendship thing works two ways. I haven't heard from you either.*

Ugh, he is so frustrating. Did he really mean to ask someone else what they were wearing? I know I shouldn't be mad, but that pisses me off. ***Go fuck yourself, Abel, and text the right person.***

Oh, kitten, how I have missed you. I'm just fucking with you. Don't get your panties all in a bunch.

I forgot how exasperating he is. I should have known better than that; he was just messing with me.

I don't wear panties. I hit send before I realize what I've typed. Shit, that's not something you tell your "friend."

I knew you wouldn't be able to resist telling me. What else are you not wearing?

I'm not going to respond to him. I've made it this long, and pushed away my feelings for him. I get up and go into the kitchen, grabbing a bottle of water and a snack. I lie back down on the couch and look at my phone. There are no more texts. Good, he got my point. Bastard.

I open my box of crackers and pop a few in my mouth. Turning the TV back on, I flip through the channels searching for something to watch. My phone vibrates again, and I grab it. Shit, now he is calling. I chew fast and answer.

"Yes."

"Kitten, why didn't you text me back?"

I take a drink of my water. "Because I don't have anything else to say to you."

"If that's really the case, then why did you answer my call?"

Geez, he's so pushy. "I didn't look at the screen; I thought it was someone else calling."

"Right. So you're telling me that you always answer your phone by saying 'yes?'"

"Jesus, you're such a pain in my ass. Just tell me what the hell you want."

He chuckles. "I want to know what you're wearing."

"Fine. If I tell you, will you leave me alone?"

"Maybe."

"In that case, you tell me first."

"I'm wearing a pair of grey sweatpants."

"And?"

"That's it, now it's your turn, kitten."

I look down at myself. "I'm wearing grey sweats as well and a red tank top."

"And?" he whispers.

"That's it."

"Do you really not wear underwear?"

"No, I don't."

"Fuck," he mutters and I hear the phone get muffled.

"Where are you?"

"In my bed. Where are you?"

"My couch," I say and yawn.

"Are you tired?"

"Mmm-hmm."

"I'll let you go then; I don't want to keep you."

No, I don't want to go; I like talking to him. I didn't realize how much I've missed him.

"No, it's okay. Why did you really call?"

He takes a deep breath. "We're having a BBQ at the station and I wanted to invite you."

"Like a date?"

"No. Not a date, as friends."

"When is it?"

"It's tomorrow afternoon."

"Can we take your bike?"

I can hear the smile in his voice. "Sure."

"Okay, I'll go."

"Good. I'll pick you up at noon?"

"That works for me."

"See you tomorrow, kitten."

"Bye," I say and hang up.

My phone rings and I scramble to answer it. "Hello?"

"Hey, how are you?" It's Alexa.

"Hey, I'm good. How are you?"

"I'm good. Vincent is at a conference this weekend and I wanted to see if we could hang out."

Shit. I don't want to lie to her, but I look at the clock; it's ten till noon. I know Abel will be here any minute and I don't have time to explain what I'm doing right now. "Yeah, that sounds great. I just got called into work, but I'm free tomorrow."

"Okay, that's perfect. Do you want me to pick you up in the morning and we can grab breakfast?"

"Yeah, that's great. I gotta run. I'll see you tomorrow."

I hang up and finish strapping my black wedge sandals. I take one final look at myself in the mirror. I'm dressed in a pair of dark skinny jeans and a black tank top. My blonde hair is flowing down my back in soft waves. I have very little makeup on, opting for a more natural look.

The doorbell rings and I fly down the stairs. I open the door and almost melt at the sight of Abel. *Damn, he looks good.* He's dressed in a pair of jeans, boots, and a leather coat. His hair is longer than the last time I saw him. He has it styled in a messy, sexy way.

"Damn, Cara. Is that really what you want to wear today?" he asks barging into my house.

"Yeah. Why?" I ask, clearly confused.

He lets out a frustrated sigh and says, "Well, for starters I'm not taking you on my bike in those shoes."

I look down at myself perplexed. "What's wrong with my shoes?"

"If we got into an accident, I don't even want to think about your feet. I was called to a fatal motorcycle accident this week, and it reminded me of how dangerous bikes can be."

"Okay, I'll change. Don't worry."

I turn to head upstairs, and Abel follows me. We enter my room and I go into my closet in search of a pair of boots. When I come out, he is standing with his hands in his pockets staring at me. I show him my leather knee high boots; they're the only pair of leather ones I have.

"They'll do for the ride, but bring your sandals too."

I nod my head. He's so bossy, and deep down I love it. I sit on the side of my bed and make quick work of taking off my sandals and putting on my boots. I stand up and then lean back down to pull the leather all the way up. When I look up at him, his jaw is clenched watching me.

"Better?" I ask standing straight and placing my hands on my hips.

"I guess, if that's all you have."

"What's your problem?"

He steps closer and looks intently into my eyes like he is searching for something. "I'm really trying here, okay? Don't you see what you're doing to me?"

I shake my head and say, "What do you mean?"

"Nothing, let's get going before we're late."

He turns and walks out of my room. *What does he mean?* Today he's so difficult to read. He needs to remember he was the one who called and invited me. I pick my sandals up off the floor and head downstairs. He's waiting for me at the front door. I don't know what to say to him, so I open the closet door to grab a hoodie.

"Don't bother, I got you something."

I look at him, surprised. "It's just a leather jacket. After the accident I saw this week I can't risk anything happening. That's why I got so pissed about your shoes."

"Thank you," I say, leaning over to give him a hug. He wraps me in his firm grip and I inhale deeply. Closing my eyes, I devour his scent. I know what I'm doing is wrong, but damn it, these feelings are so hard to fight. He pulls away from me and I slowly open my eyes. Ever so gently, he takes his fingers pushing the hair out of my eyes and behind my ear. I swallow hard and want him to kiss me. My body is a mess of raging hormones. He grabs my hand and we walk out of my condo towards his awaiting Harley. His grip is firm and I like how his hand feels around mine. Walking up to his bike, he opens one of the saddlebags and pulls out a cute little black leather jacket. I take it from him in exchange for my shoes, which he places in the bag. I slide the jacket on; it fits perfectly. I zip it up and look to him for approval.

"Damn, you look good in leather."

"Thank you, it's perfect."

"Of course. I'm glad it fits; they only had one size small left."

He hands me my helmet, which I quickly get on, and then wrap my hair into a large bun at the base of my neck.

"Ready?" he asks. I nod my head and we climb on the bike. As he pulls out, I think about lying to Alexa. I don't know why I didn't just tell her that I was going with Abel. I guess part of me doesn't want to hear her motherly lecture. I know it's coming; I gave it to her when she started seeing Vincent. But what am I talking about? I'm not seeing Abel, nor am I going to. We are two friends going to a BBQ. I'm thinking too hard about all of this and my head hurts already from the mind fuck I'm giving myself. I need a drink; I can tell it's going to be one of those kinds of days.

Chapter 5

Morning After

I open my eyes but my vision is blurry and my head hurts. I clamp my eyes shut and pull the covers over my head. I realize as I lie there that I have a hangover. Damn it, I hate hangovers. I try again to open my eyes, this time with my head tucked underneath the covers. Once I manage to pull my vision into focus I notice that my sheets are dark gray. *What the hell?* I pull the covers back and blink wildly looking around. I'm not in my room. Shit, where am I? I look next to me and no one else is in the bed. I go to get up and my clothes are thrown all over the floor.

Motherfucker.

Think, Cara, think. What happened? I remember being at the BBQ, and I started taking shots with Troy. I sit up and look around but there is no sign of Abel. Quietly, I get out of bed and leave the bedroom. Once I reach the living room I'm stopped dead in my tracks.

Sleeping peacefully on the couch is Abel. He is naked from the waist up and his body is almost covered in tattoos. I thought it was just his arms, but they're everywhere. I step closer wanting to get a better look at his art when the floor creaks. His sleepy eyes open and he looks at me. I smile shyly at him, not able to remember what happened last night.

"How are you feeling?" he asks.

I shake my head, and realize I feel like I'm going to pass out. He sits up and pats the couch next to him. I walk over and sit down. Looking at myself I suddenly realize I'm wearing one of his Denver Fire t-shirts and nothing else. Sitting down, I go to grab a pillow to pull on my lap, but he covers me with the blanket he was using instead.

Abel gets up, and as he walks by, I can't miss the hard on he has. I look up at him and he puts his hand over it.

"It's just morning wood, kitten. Don't worry. Nothing like that happened last night."

He walks off and goes into what I assume is the bathroom. Holy shit, his dick is huge. Alexa told me Vincent was hung, but I never thought about Abel being big as well. Clearly he is, because I've never seen anything like that before. I pull my knees up to my chest and rest my head on them. I close my eyes to try and make my head stop throbbing.

I hear the door open and I look at Abel as he comes

out of the bathroom. His hair is wet and I assume that he splashed himself with water.

"Have you thrown up any more?" he asks.

Shit, I threw up? "No."

"You're not a morning person are you?"

"I normally am, but I hate having a hangover. It's the worst feeling in the world."

"I know it is. I tried to tell you last night to slow down, but there was no stopping you."

"What happened?"

"You don't remember?"

I shake my head and he comes from the kitchen with a glass of water and a handful of pills. "Take these."

I look at the six pills he hands me and don't question him in the slightest. I knock them back and slam the entire glass of water.

"I'll give you the shortened version, okay?"

I nod my head again and an orange tabby cat jumps into his lap. It lies down and he automatically pets it as he speaks. "You and Troy thought it would be a good idea to see who could outdrink who. One thing led to another and after hours of beer pong and I don't know how many shots, you could barely stand. I obviously couldn't take you home on the bike, so we walked here since the BBQ was at the station. I planned on taking you home in my truck, but then you started to throw up. After that, let's just say your hormones kicked in and you pulled out every trick in the book to try and get me into bed with you. Trust me, I wanted you so bad, I wished someone would've just killed me. But I wouldn't do that to you. At least, not until you tell me when you're clearheaded that you want me."

I swallow hard, feeling all of the color rush to my face. I'm blushing like I've never blushed before. Abel smirks at me, and I bury my head in my knees. His cat comes over to me and starts to rub on my arm. I look at the cat and it meows at me. "I know, Puss; I feel the same way," Abel says.

"You named your cat Puss?" I ask.

"Yup, I did. So pet Puss, then we're going to eat."

Answer your phone twat-waffle. I look down at my phone reading the text as Abel drives me home. I forgot I had plans with Alexa this morning, and we were supposed to eat breakfast. Well, now it's almost noon so she's going to have to settle for lunch.

Abel pulls his black Ford truck in front of my condo and I turn to him. "Thank you for last night. I'm sorry if I embarrassed you or did anything stupid."

He turns towards me with his eyebrows creased and rests his elbow on the center console. "You could never embarrass me, and last night you were far from stupid."

I smile at him and open my door. "Thanks for

saying that. I'll talk to you soon."

"Yes, you will."

As I shut my door, my phone rings and I look down at it. It's Alexa and I know she is in full-blown crazy mode. I walk off from Abel towards my condo and answer her call.

"Hey, Lex."

"What the hell, Cara, are you okay?"

"Yeah, I'm alright. I think I may have eaten something bad last night, because I feel like shit and didn't sleep well."

"Oh no, I'm sorry. Well, I guess breakfast is out of the question?"

I can't help but laugh at her. "Lex, it's almost noon."

"You're right; it is. Okay, well, let's try and get together this week for dinner? I have a hair appointment this afternoon or I would say we could hang out later."

"That's okay, dinner sounds great."

"Do you need me to bring you anything?"

"No, thanks, I'm going to take a nap. I'll text you later."

"Feel better. Bye."

I hang up and walk into my room to shower. I slowly peel my clothes off, still feeling bone-tired. I wonder how I got undressed last night. Did Abel do it for me?

The water is hot, and I wash my body just wanting to crawl into bed. Running my hands over my breasts, I can't stop myself from going farther down and touching in between my legs. Fuck, it has been too long since I've been with anyone. I start to rub slow circles, and then stop when I hear my phone ring. I rinse and get out looking at the screen. It was Abel. I call him right back.

"Sorry, I was in the shower," I say as he answers.

"No biggie. I just wanted to check in on you and see how you're feeling."

"I'm okay, just tired."

"Are you still in your towel?" he asks.

"Yes. Why do you always want to know what I'm wearing?"

"Drop your towel, Cara," he commands.

I look around my room like he's here. Unsure as to why I am even considering doing this, I drop it. My breathing is quick, and he has my body tingling.

"Did you do it?"

"Mmm-hmm."

"Good, now lie on your bed."

Again listening to his commands, I walk to the bed and sit down. Lying backwards, I stretch my naked body across the cool, white fabric.

I can hear his deep breathing into the phone. "Close your eyes and listen to me. Take your hands and caress your breasts. I want you to squeeze them just how you want me to do it for you." I keep my mouth closed to try and muffle the noises wanting to escape me.

"With the tips of yours fingers, pinch your nipples

49

imagining that my body is lying on top of yours. I'm going to take my mouth and wrap it around one of your hard, pink nipples. I know they're pink like your lips, Cara."

I can't stop myself from moaning into the phone as I touch myself. It's as though he's here with me.

"Good girl. Now take your other hand and slide it down your body. I want you to slowly explore every curve of yourself. Remember this is me doing this to you."

"Mmm-hmm," I say as my left hand teases my nipple and my other slowly moves, gliding over my rib cage then to my hip.

"Don't touch yourself until I tell you," he murmurs.

"What are you doing?" I whisper.

"I'm unzipping my pants and I'm going to grab my cock. I can feel your lips on me as you lick and suck the head while I squeeze the base. Your lips are so soft as they move up and down. I'm taking my free hand to touch your pussy. I want you to slowly spread your swollen lips and show me how you want me to touch you."

"Fuck, Abel," I cry into the phone.

"Yes, baby, just like that. Show me how you like it. How do you want me to make you come?"

I start to whimper and cry as my body is close to orgasm. I hear his breathing become fast and harsh as we both pleasure each other. The feeling is so strong it is as though we are not doing this over the phone.

"Come with me, Cara," he growls into the phone.

I let go, crying loudly. I scream his name rubbing myself aggressively. Abel grunts and I know he is coming too. Once my body stops convulsing, I feel a little embarrassed.

"Fuck, that was good, Cara. I want you so bad; imagine how good we could be together."

"I know, but I can't risk getting hurt again."

Chapter 6

What's New?

I ring the doorbell and wait outside of Alexa and Vincent's house. We're having dinner tonight and I came prepared with dessert and a bottle of Alexa's favorite wine. She opens the door and has the biggest smile on her face when she sees me.

"Hey, doll," she says and wraps me in a big hug.

I walk into their home and notice the smell immediately. Vincent is in the kitchen with his back to us cooking away. "Hey, Vincent," I say. He turns around and gives me a side hug. He is so brotherly and I love him for that.

"Thank you guys for having me."

"Of course," Alexa says. "So tell us what's new with you."

I shake my head because the first thing that pops into my mind is Abel. I'm not going to tell them about the BBQ, and I'm sure as hell not telling them about the phone sex. "I'm not here to talk about me. Tell me all about the proposal — did he get down on one knee, and do you love the ring?"

Her face lights up thinking back on things with Vincent. "Cara, it was perfect, our room was all set up with white rose petals and candles. And yes, you know how he is, of course he got down on one knee."

I squeal with happiness for my best friend. "Let me see your ring"

She happily shows me the oval cut diamond that I act like I've never seen before. "It's beautiful," I gush.

"Alright, ladies, let's eat," Vincent interrupts us and walks by with a pan of deliciousness.

Both Alexa and I hop up from the kitchen island and go into the dining room.

"So, Cara, have you seen Abel at all lately?" Vincent asks.

I freeze midair with a forkful of food. "Nope. Why do you ask?"

"He has just made it extremely clear lately that he's interested in you, so I wanted to see how you were handling that battle."

I laugh and try to think of what to say. "There's no battle there. I haven't seen or talked to him in a while. I told you both, I'm over guys like him. I'm not willing to put my heart out there and get it hurt again."

"Good. I think that's smart of you. Since college, he hasn't has a steady girlfriend and everything I know about the girls he's been with since is basically a horror story of a string of hookups that he's used for sex or whatever else he wanted. Cara, you're like a sister to me; I don't want to see you get hurt."

I smile at Vincent, but on the inside I feel sick. It hurts to hear that Abel only uses women. But it's all the confirmation I need to know that I'm making the right decision.

"Well, enough about Abel. I want to hear about you two. How is it living together and being engaged? Vincent, have you cracked her bitchy morning attitude yet?"

They look at one another and he drapes his arm over her shoulder. "I'm still working on the whole morning situation. As long as I keep my phone quiet and wake her up with Starbucks, she's happy."

I watch my best friend smile from ear to ear. Vincent completes her, he makes her whole, and with him she is truly happy. I've never wanted anything more for her than this. She has been through so much hurt and pain in her life; she really deserves her happily ever after. I hope one day I can have mine.

My fingers fly over the keyboard of my phone as I text Bridgette, Alexa's spunky little sister. I look at the time and I have ten minutes left of my break before I have to head back to work. She texted me about staying with me after she graduates, and I think it's a fabulous idea. I'm really excited to have a roommate again and I adore Bridgette, so it's an ideal situation.

I throw my sandwich wrapper away and run right smack dab into Ben. "Oh my gosh, are you okay?" I ask as coffee spills out the top of his cup and onto his hand.

"Yeah. I'm fine," he says and licks the coffee off of his skin.

"Listen, I never got a chance to apologize for how my friend acted. Every time I came to talk, you were busy with a patient. I'm really sorry, he had no right to attack you like that. Can you forgive me and I'll buy you lunch, this time it'll be my treat?"

He looks at me with a curious expression. "So he's not your boyfriend?"

"Oh God, no! He's just a really good friend and can be overprotective."

"Fine, but you're not paying. I am."

I nod my head. "Okay, does Monday work?"

"Yeah, I'll see you then."

I glance at the clock on my phone. "Sorry, I gotta run. See you next week."

He waves at me and I leave him behind heading back into the ER. Jamie is updating our patient board when I return.

"Alright, girl, I'm back. You can go to lunch," I say.

"Great, I'm starving. I'll see you in a bit."

I smile at her as she walks off. Sitting at my computer, I keep busy checking my e-mail and the status of my orders. Rarely are things this quiet in here, and quite frankly I don't know if I like the silence. I fill out a few of my charts before I get up to start my rounds.

I walk into room 112 and sitting on the chair next to the bed is a small, elderly woman. She has her head down and looks to be crying. She is tightly gripping the hand of the man lying in the bed. When I look at him I realize his color is gone and he has passed away.

I walk around to her and gently place my hand on her back. She turns to look at me as if she hadn't noticed I was in the room.

"Hey. Can I get you anything?"

She shakes her head and more tears wash over her eyes. I don't say anything else; all I can do is just stand there with her. After about ten minutes, I leave her to go and inform all of the proper people. I return to her side with a cup of tea, and she hasn't moved.

"Here, I brought this for you. It's important you take care of yourself during a time like this."

She takes the tea from me. "Thank you, dear," she says.

"Of course. I'm *so* sorry for your loss."

"It's okay, sweetie. Fred and I were together for sixty-five years. I wouldn't change a day of the time we shared. We knew one day this would happen. This isn't goodbye; I'll see him again one day."

"Wow, sixty-five years. That's amazing, congratulations."

"Thank you. Do you have a husband?"

I shake my head.

"Well, why not?"

"I don't know. I always seem to fall for the wrong guys."

She smiles at me and sets her tea down. She finally lets go of her husband's hand and grabs mine. "Don't worry, dear, it will happen and most likely when you least expect it. Just follow your heart; it'll *never* steer you wrong."

"Thanks for saying that. I hope my day will come." I continue on my way, so she can spend some time with her husband alone before he is taken away. The rest of my day flies by; things pick up and we do end up getting really busy. Before I know it, I'm debriefing the night crew.

Walking out of the hospital my body feels spent. I'm so tired that I just want to sleep in my car, but I can't, so I drive home. On the drive, my mind drifts to Abel. I have to admit to myself that I miss him, and I miss him a lot. I find myself wondering why he hasn't called, but I guess I should be glad he seems to be backing off. It's better this way, right? After what Vincent told me, I know keeping it platonic is definitely the safest option. Deep down, I repeatedly tell myself that things will not go any further, hoping to control the spiraling feelings inside of me.

The woman tonight told me to follow my heart, and before I know it I'm going against the logic of my mind and doing just that. I pick up my phone and dial Abel's number. He doesn't answer. I know I should leave a message, but I don't.

I pull into the garage and head inside. I can't wait until Bridgette lives here; coming home every night alone is getting old. I change out of my scrubs and into some pajamas. I really should shower after working all day, but I decide that I'll do it tomorrow.

I stretch out on the couch and call Abel again. He doesn't answer, so I call my sister. I haven't talked to her in what feels like forever. While we talk I tinker around with my iPad and she rambles on about a new guy she's into and then my battery dies. Shit, I hate cell phones. She was just about to tell me about a date she went on the other night, and then nothing. To add to my annoyance, these stupid phones take at least ten minutes to boot back up. Since I'm feeling lazy and can e-mail her from my iPad, I do and tell her, *I'm sorry my phone died.* I'll charge it later or when I head to bed.

Getting comfy on the couch, I flip on the TV to an episode of *The Deadliest Catch*. As I watch it my eyelids get heavy, and just as I drift off, the doorbell rings causing me to jump. *Who the hell is coming here so late?* I really wish I had a roommate here during times like this. I look out the peephole. With his head down, I can see it's Abel. I unlock the door, causing his head jerk up and he looks into my eyes. I can see the worry on his face. He again is covered in soot and looks exhausted.

"Hey, are you okay?" I ask.

"I'm fine. I was worried when you wouldn't pick up your phone. I've been trying to call you for almost an hour."

I open the door all the way and he walks inside. "I'm sorry. I was on the phone with my sister and then the stupid battery died."

He is dressed in his cargo pants and Denver Fire t-shirt. It looks like he hasn't slept for a week. "Are you sure you're okay?" I ask.

"Yeah. We've been rotating twenty-hour shifts on a wildfire down south. This is the first time I've been back to the city in a week. I can't wait to shower and eat a good meal, but I wanted to check on you first."

"Why don't you shower here and I'll cook for you?"

"Really?"

"Yes, really. I'll wash your clothes for you if you want."

"You don't have to do that. I have a bag in my truck."

"Perfect. Go get in the shower and I'll cook. Do you want anything in particular?"

He looks at me with a grin on his face. "Nothing special, kitten. Just food and a lot of it."

I go into the kitchen and inspect what I have so I can make him a good meal. I realize then I haven't eaten dinner either. He walks back in with his bag over his shoulder.

"You can use my bathroom; it's in my room. There are towels under the sink."

"Thanks," he says and walks upstairs.

I turn my attention back to the fridge and off of his perfect ass. I decide on making us some Italian subs, and since I have some leftover noodles, I make my version of an antipasto salad.

Just as I cut the sandwiches in half, Abel walks downstairs wearing a clean white t-shirt with his tattoos faintly visible through the fabric and a pair of black shorts.

"Is it okay with you if we eat on the couch?" I ask him.

"Of course. Do you need help with anything?"

"Nope. You sit and relax."

He flops down on the sofa and I can see the exhaustion on his face. I walk over holding our drinks in my hands and balance the plates on top of the cups. I hand him his and he takes it and then takes mine.

"Are these Italian subs?" he asks.

"Yup, is that okay?"

"Is that okay? These are my all-time favorite. When it's my turn to cook at the station, I just order Jimmy Johns."

"Good. Well, I hope you like them." I cross my legs underneath me and watch Abel as he devours his sandwich. I can barely finish half of mine when his plate is clean.

"Do you want my other half?"

"Sure, if you're not going to finish it."

I shake my head and he takes it off of my plate, again devouring it. I finish my antipasto and put my plate on the table in front of us.

"Was it good?" I ask.

"It was the best, way better than Jimmy John's. Next time I have to cook at the station, you have to come down and make these for the guys. They'll love them."

"Okay. I would be happy to."

"I'm going to hold you to that."

He leans over and encloses me in his arms, hugging me tightly to his warm body. "Thank you for the food and the shower."

"You don't have to thank me. It's nice to see you. I've missed you."

He tilts his head to the side and looks from my eyes to my lips. He leans back into the sofa pulling me along with him. I comply and stretch my body along his. Once we're laid back, he wraps his other arm around me and I rest my cheek on his chest, looking at the colors from his tattoos, as they force their way to the surface through the light fabric. I trace my finger over a heart I can see that says 'Mom.' I remember Alexa telling me how Abel and

Vincent lost their mom in a tragic car accident about five years ago.

Neither of us speaks and I enjoy the quiet time in his arms. As I rest my hand on his chest, I realize that his nipples are pierced. The pressure from my fingers shows the barbells straining against the fabric. This time, I can't resist and I lean up lifting his t-shirt so I can see everything that's underneath.

The detail is exquisite; his tattoos are a beautiful mixture of color and black and gray. Some are pictures while others are script. I can't stop my hand from touching him. As soon as my fingers press into his hard skin, he freezes. His breathing stops and he is watching my hand.

"Is this okay?" I whisper.

He looks at me letting out the breath he was holding. Nodding his head he reaches up and cups the back of my head. I lean into his touch and let him pull me to him. My face is only inches from his.

"I'm going to kiss you, Cara."

I don't speak, I don't hesitate, instead I move my lips to meet his. The instant our mouths touch, a flame erupts within me. *Finally*. His lips are soft and warm, a heady combination. He moves them slowly over mine and tightly grips my hair. I moan a little as he sucks on my bottom lip. My hands explore his body, feeling every curve and contour of him. Each bump of his six-pack moves beneath my fingers like ridges of a mountain. I continue exploring him until I get to the waistband of his shorts.

I want to put my hand inside so badly. *God, I want him; I need him.* I resist and straddle him instead, pressing my body firmly against his. In between my legs his erection is present and large; it makes my mouth go mad. I take over the kiss and am no longer being patient or gentle. I part his lips with my tongue and caress his, really feeling what it's like to kiss him. It has been so long that we've waited for this, and I can't question him any longer. My mind has insisted it's wrong, but my heart is screaming this is so right.

His hands are resting on my hips holding my body, and I need more of him. I pull back and look into his eyes. Lying beneath me, his eyelids are heavy. I stare at him as he breathes, taking deep breaths and keeping my body in a vice grip against his.

"Cara, I need you to tell me what you want. I don't want you to regret any of this."

"Abel, I want you."

"Are you sure?"

I nod my head and he flips us over, so I'm now pinned underneath him. He holds his weight off of me, leaning back down to kiss me. This time he is aggressive. He shows no mercy with me and controls the kiss just how he wants it. I slide my hands up his back, under his shirt and rake my fingernails down his back. "Will you take this off?" I ask.

He sits up and removes his t-shirt throwing it across the room. I grab his biceps and pull myself up into him as I remove my shirt. He looks down at my perky breasts and grabs them, feeling and caressing the hardened mounds. He doesn't waste a second exploring my nipples with his fingers.

"I knew your nipples were pink like your lips. I bet your pussy is just as pink."

I lift my hips and shimmy down my pants. He helps me take them all the way off, but doesn't rush what we're doing. He comes back to kiss me, and boy, does he kiss me. The possession he takes of my mouth is like nothing I've ever felt before. His tongue is strong, yet gentle. Everything about him is incredible. His right hand leaves my breast and moves down my rib cage and then across my stomach. Once he reaches my sex, he looks at me with pure lust.

"I need you to tell me what you want."

"I already told you."

"Tell me again, Cara. Tell me how much you want me."

"Please, Abel, I need you. You're all I think about."

He dips a finger between my wet pussy lips and stops moving, asking. "How much?"

"Fuck. A lot. Okay? Please don't make me wait any longer."

His skilled fingers work magic on my clit, circling and moving in just the right way to make me crazy.

Slowly, he glides his finger inside of me and moves it in and out.

"Fuck, baby, you're so tight. I don't know if I'll fit."

"You'll fit," I moan as he slides a second finger inside of me.

"That's it, stretch for me," he says. His movements expand my already swollen pussy. With each movement of his hand, I move my hips matching his rhythm. He moves down the couch so he is kneeling between my legs. With his fingers still inside of me, he nestles his mouth around my clit. The feeling of both sensations combined makes me want to come. He pulls his mouth away and watches his fingers move in and out of me.

I lean up on my elbows and look at him as he kisses the inside of my thigh. Pulling his fingers out, he lies back on top of me and looks deep into my eyes.

"Are you sure you want to do this?"

I nod my head.

"Do you have any condoms?"

"No! Do you?"

He shakes his head.

"Damn it, Abel! You're the one with a penis. How do you not have a condom?"

He scratches his head. "I don't know. I always use them, but when I met you I threw them all out. I thought that we would never get to do this, and I haven't wanted anybody else. You made it pretty clear that you'd put me in the friend zone."

"Damn it," I snap and throw myself back into the couch.

He leans over me and asks, "Are you on birth control?"

"Yeah."

"Well, then we don't need one," he says and kisses my neck. He continues in between kisses, "Plus, I want to feel your pussy without anything separating us."

I nod my head, because it's true — I am on the pill and I want him, more than I've ever wanted anything in my life. I watch as he stands to remove his shorts. Holy shit, he is right; I don't know if he will fit inside of me. I sit up to get a better look at him. He moves closer to me and I love that his thighs are tattooed. I don't waste a second grabbing him and jerking his cock up and down. As a small drop of cum escapes the tip, I lick it up before it drips off.

"Fuck, I didn't expect that," he murmurs.

"You have no idea. Watch this."

I slide his massive cock into my mouth and am pissed that it won't go all the way down. I don't have a gag reflex, but his length and my throat just don't match. I move up and down as far as I can. My eyes are closed and I love every minute of finally being able to do this with him.

"Damn, kitten, you're about to make me come."

I stop and look up at him. His brows are creased and he looks exhausted.

"Sit down," I say and pat the couch next to me.

He does so and I climb on top of him. He reaches between us and guides his dick inside of me as I lower my body onto him. He fits. He's huge and it's tight, but fuck, it feels so good. Once he's buried as far in me as he can go I wrap my arms around his neck.

Facing him, I move up, all the while his hands explore my body helping to lead me. I can't help but moan and make noises; I've never felt anything like this before. Looking into my eyes, he pulls me to him. My lips hit his and we get lost kissing and fucking each other. Abel makes the sexiest noise as we fuck. It's a low, deep moan and I know he's enjoying what we're doing.

I slam my body harder on him, but it's not enough. I need more; I want to feel all of him.

"Harder," I demand.

He stops and lifts me off of him. Turning me around he directs me to kneel on the couch. "You like it rough, Cara? Bend over and I'll give it to you harder."

I bend over. Now on all fours with him behind me, slowly he fills me, and then pulls back out. He keeps the rhythm steady and I want more. I clench my pussy muscles tightly around him and he stops.

"Don't do that, or I'll come, baby."

"Then fuck me hard, Abel."

He reaches for my breasts, pulling me up, my back against his chest. I'm still kneeling on the couch and he has my body pressed against his. He begins to move and I wrap my arms around his neck behind me, pulling his mouth to mine. Finally turning away I try not to come. Every move he makes pushes me millimeters away from shattering.

"You like it when I fuck you rough?"

I mumble and cry again, calling his name trying to hold onto my release. "Fuck," I scream and let go. Abel's moans turn to grunts as he pounds me so hard he almost lifts me off the couch. Letting go, he comes inside of me and is relentless in his release.

Finally slowing his movements, his mouth finds my body, kissing everywhere he can touch. I run my fingers through his hair, and love that he is letting it grow.

"Fuck, Cara, that was so good."

"Mhh," is the only thing I can get out. Abel pulls out of me and I turn to kiss him before heading into the bathroom. When I come out, he is dressed and has his bag on his shoulder.

"Where are you going?" I demand.

"Home. I'm beat, kitten, and I need to sleep."

I shake my head and open the front door. Damn it, he used me, just like Vincent told me he would. I wave my hand in the direction of outside, so he knows I want him to leave. His mouth is in a thin, straight line as he walks up to me grabbing me by my waist.

"What's wrong?"

"Just go. Vincent told me you would do this and I was dumb enough to let it happen."

"Vincent told you I would do what?"

"That you would use me like you have every other woman. Please just leave, Abel. This was a mistake."

He slams the door and drops his bag to the floor. Stepping closer, he is inches away from my face. His brow is furrowed and I can tell he is pissed.

"What we did tonight was not a mistake. Why would you even say that?"

"Abel, I'm not going to be another girl you can just use. I have needs too and if you can't give me what I need, then I'll find someone who can."

"What else do you want? If you want me to fuck you again, I will."

I shake my head as tears well up in my eyes, "Please just go."

He grabs my face and forces me to look into his hazel eyes. I can see genuine concern within them. "I'm not leaving. Tell me what you need. I'll do anything."

I feel foolish for saying the words, but I want to sleep in his arms. "Stay the night with me?"

He nods his head and locks the front door. Taking my hand he leads me upstairs and to my bedroom. "Are you sure you want to stay?"

"Yes, Cara, I am."

He takes his shirt off and I get undressed. I always sleep naked and he has seen all of me, so I'm not embarrassed. I get into bed and lift the covers for him. He seems to hesitate and then slides in. I nestle myself in the crook of his arm and enjoy having him here. I never thought in a million years we would be in this place and now that we finally are, I feel so complete.

"I'm sorry if you thought I was leaving because of you. I haven't stayed with a woman in over a decade. Sex has always been a means to an end; we took our pleasure and parted ways. I don't know how to do this. Honestly, my instinct to leave was out of habit, not because I'm done with you. I'm far from done with you."

"I'm not done with you either, Abel."

He rests his hand on the side of my hip and kisses the top of my head. Neither of us speaks again and I listen as his breathing slows. I look up at his eyes and I can tell he is asleep. I rest my chin on his chest and watch him, sleeping peacefully. I lean up and turn the lamp off on my nightstand kissing his lips one more time. I nestle down, getting comfy in his arms and quickly drift off.

Chapter 7

Sex

I wake and next to me, Abel is lying in the same spot he fell asleep. I have since moved off of him and onto my stomach in the middle of the bed. I watch him sleep and know that he is exhausted. I couldn't imagine working twenty hours straight every day for a week. So I let him rest and gently kiss him before getting out of bed. He needs to sleep as long as he can and since I know he likes to eat, I'm going to make him breakfast.

I slide on his discarded t-shirt so if he comes down while I'm cooking, he will be shirtless. My first order of business in the kitchen is coffee. Once I have that brewing, I grab the ingredients for breakfast. I put on the bacon and turn on my iPod. 'Some Nights' by fun. is playing and I think back to last night — it was quite a night. Mind-blowing could sum it up. I crack the eggs and whip them up for French toast. I pull the griddle out and turn it on, dip the bread, and lay each piece onto the hot metal. I see Abel emerge from my room at the top of the stairs. I can tell he is groggy, but he smiles at me and slowly comes down the stairs.

"Good morning, kitten," he says. Once he reaches me, he wraps his arms around me. I turn to face him and kiss his lips. He tastes good.

"Good morning to you. Do you want coffee?"

"Please. Is this for real right now?"

"Yeah, why do you ask?"

"I just never thought this would happen. And to think my dumb ass tried to leave last night."

"You're not dumb, but I'm glad you stayed," I say and kiss him, turning back around to attend to cooking our food.

"Me too, especially because I can do this," as he takes his hand and snakes it between my legs, dipping a finger inside me. I tilt my head back and enjoy the pleasure.

"Holy shit, that feels good."

"Wait till I eat, and then watch what I'm going to do to you."

"Why do we have to eat first?"

"I need energy, because I plan on fucking you all day. This may be the only meal we get in."

"I can cook while you fuck me."

He pulls his finger out of me. "No, you can't. Cara, you like it rough, therefore cooking and sex is not a good mix."

"I've never had sex any other way. That's all I know."

"Me too, that's why we work so well together. But I want to savor each time I'm inside you. So maybe we should try to take things slow after we eat."

"You can do anything you want to me."

"Anything?" he asks and bites my neck.

"Mmm-hmm."

"Hurry up with our food then, because I can't wait much longer."

I hand Abel two coffee cups, while I pile our plates with food and set them on the breakfast bar.

"How do you like your coffee?" he asks.

"A little cream and sugar, please."

Once we both sit to eat, I look over at him and his stomach is ridiculous, the muscles are so toned and he has some tattoos on them. I wonder what caused him to get all of his artwork done.

He looks at me with a mouthful of food. "What?"

"Nothing," I say and take a bite of my delicious French toast.

"Don't look at me like that. I told you I need to eat."

"Well, maybe you should put some clothes on."

He turns to me. "I'm sorry, but you stole my shirt."

I glare at him. He isn't going to flip this back on me. "With or without a shirt, I can't keep myself from staring."

"Really? Why have you been fighting this then?"

"I don't know. I guess 'cause I've never had a good relationship. I've been hurt and cheated on so many times that I lost count. And to be honest, I pre-judged you."

"Well, I'm glad we've moved past that. All I can give you is me, and I hope that's enough."

"I don't need anything more; just don't hurt me."

"I won't. I promise."

I look at him as lust fills me. He is so fucking sexy. "I guess I should give this back to you," I say pulling his t-shirt over my head.

Before I can do anything else he lifts me off of my bar stool and I wrap my legs around his waist. Looking in his eyes I can tell there is nothing in that moment that would stop him. Not that I want him too.

"Jesus, your fucking body is perfect," he says, squeezing my ass.

I tilt my head back as his fingers dig into my skin. He leans into my neck, kissing and sucking on the exposed skin. I wrap my arms tightly around him. I love the way he kisses, and how he makes noises as he does so. Reaching down, I push his shorts off causing them to fall to the floor.

My breathing is ragged, as is his. I can feel his dick resting against me, and before I can move to try and get him inside of me, he sets me on the kitchen counter. Looking down at him, he moves and rests my legs on his shoulders. Then slowly, oh so slowly, he moves his mouth to my sex, kissing all around and finally securing his warm lips around my throbbing clit. The feeling sends my body into mania. *Fuck, he's good with his mouth.*

He moves his tongue back and forth and then dips it inside of me. I reach for his head, gripping his hair and pulling him closer to me. The feeling pushes me close to coming and I pull away. He looks at me, confused. "What's wrong, baby?"

I shake my head a little embarrassed.

"Tell me," he whispers.

"I don't want to come yet."

He pulls me closer to him and creases his eyebrows. "I'm going to make you come more than once, Cara. Let go and enjoy the sensation; I told you I'm going to fuck you all day."

I've never been with a man and orgasmed more than once. But I can tell he's serious, and I can't wait to fuck him all day. I kiss him tasting myself on his mouth. He holds his arm firmly around my body and moves from kissing my mouth to my jaw, down my neck, to my collarbone, finally landing on a nipple. He grabs it with his lips and sucks, pulling up. The feeling causes me to moan and lean into his touch.

His erection is hot and moist as it presses against me, and I want him inside of me. I reach between us and grab him. Abel stops torturing my breasts and looks at me. I tug him and guide him towards my pussy. He shakes his head and says, "Not yet."

I let go of him and throw my head back, looking to the ceiling. Damn it, I need to calm the ache between my legs. It's like he can read my thoughts, moving his sweet lips back to my clit. The instant he touches me, my body convulses, spiraling into oblivion. Everything inside of me is on fire. I try to pull away from the intensity, but he grips my body pulling me hard against him.

Once he finally releases the pressure, I feel like I can breathe again. Looking down at him, he looks up at me and says, "Fuck, you're delicious."

"I bet you taste just as good." I slide off of the counter and kiss his neck, continuing my trail of kisses down his chest until I reach his pierced nipples. I lick all around them, enjoying playing with the metal. Taking my hand, I fiercely clutch his cock, making him moan in appreciation.

Dropping to my knees I indulge in my new favorite pastime and push away any worry or angst I have about being with Abel. I know it comes with the possibility of heartache, but he promised he wouldn't hurt me, and I'm already in too deep — I have to believe him. Cupping his tight balls in my right hand, and wrapping my other hand around to his ass I grip it, sucking him hard, up and down, hands free.

He rubs the backs of his fingers down my face, causing me to look up at him, loving the sweet gesture. His moans intensify and he starts to move in and out of my mouth. Releasing his balls, I take my other hand and grip his ass. Kneeling in front of him, I hold onto him and move as fast as I can.

"Fuck, baby," he gasps, exploding into my mouth. I swallow and continue to suck him, holding him to me, the same way he did when I came. I feel his body twitch and I know I'm driving him crazy. Looking up at him, he bites his lip and I can tell he wants more.

I stand up, and immediately he turns me around, bending me down onto the cool countertop. "You drive my body absolutely fucking insane. Maybe later we'll try and go slow, but right now I'm going to make you scream."

The anticipation is almost too much for me to handle. My body is tense, waiting for him to be inside of me. I look back at him just as he steps closer to me, nudging the head of his cock against my opening. All of my blood rushes there, waiting for him to enter, needing him to.

"Are you ready, baby?"

I nod my head and he slams into me. It feels unbelievable. His hands wrap around the front of my thighs as he moves. I can't help but cry out his name, which only makes him fuck me harder. I rest up on my forearms as we move our bodies together. His breathing is harsh, and his noises are low and deep.

I want to touch him, so I start standing up. He immediately pulls out of me, and I turn around, wrapping my arms around his muscular neck. He lifts me onto the counter and nuzzles back inside of my wet core. Grabbing my face with both of his hands he sinks his tongue into my mouth, teasing and tantalizing mine as he fucks me.

I finally stop kissing him, looking into his heat-filled eyes. I lean onto the counter top, my back pressed against the cold surface. He is holding my hip with his left hand and his right hand is splayed across my belly. I love how he is moving his hips in a rhythm almost on top of me.

"Are you ready to come again?" he asks in between breaths.

I shake my head not wanting this to end. Abel creases his brows and moves his thumb to my clit. I watch him enjoy observing moving in and out of me. He's watching our bodies, and I let go, coming hard. The moment I fall into desertion, he does the same. My body is hot and I'm out of breath. I look to Abel, all sweaty and glistening.

"Why are you looking at me like that?" he asks.

"No reason."

Lifting me into his arms, he tightly holds me to his chest. "Tell me."

"I've never had sex like that."

He kisses me behind the ear and says, "Oh, kitten, you have no idea what I can do to you. We're just getting started."

Chapter 8

Rockies

"Will you stop distracting me so I can finish getting ready?" I say to Abel. We are at his house and about to head out to the Colorado Rockies baseball game. He won't keep his hands off of me and we are already running late. We planned on eating dinner before the game, but that's not going to happen.

I'm applying my makeup sitting on his bed in nothing but a towel. I try not to watch him as he moves around the room in just his Hugo Boss underwear. What I want to do is peel them off of him and fuck him senseless. He looks over at me and I quickly look away. He just chuckles, and I drool over his legs — they're so toned and muscular — and his back is insane. The definition of his muscles rippling through not only his skin, but also his tattoos, is so sexy.

"Cara, you're driving me mad. You need to stop eye-fucking me, or we're not going to make it to the game."

I put my hand over my chest innocently. "I'm driving you mad? You're the one who is strutting around here practically naked. I'm doing everything I can to contain my drool and not say fuck the game."

"Oh, we're going to the game, so stop eye-fucking me and hurry up, woman."

I can't help but laugh at him, he's so funny. I finish my makeup and scrunch my hair, leaving it messy and down, just pulling my bangs back. I quickly dress in jeans and my favorite jersey. Of course I love the Diamondbacks — they're my home team — and tonight that's who the Rockies are playing. Growing up in Arizona, my dad took me to a lot of their games. Abel, being a Colorado native, is a huge Rockies fan. As I walk out of his bedroom, he is ready, checking his hat in the mirror.

"Damn. As much as I hate the Diamondbacks, you look hot as hell in red. Plus, it is my favorite color."

I look up at him and grab the sides of his jersey, pulling his lips to mine. "You look hot as hell too, even in a Rockies jersey."

He kisses me so softly, and I love it. Grabbing my hand, we leave and head out of his building. It's a warm night and both of us decide to skip bringing a coat or hoodie. Since Abel lives in the heart of downtown, we walk to the game.

The closer we get to the stadium, the bigger the crowds, the more intense the energy. The fans are all crazy and excited, and most are drunk. I feel Abel tighten his grip on my hand and when I look over at him, he's scanning the crowd while we walk. I love how protective he is watching everyone and ensuring that we stay safe.

I slide my arm around his waist, and he drapes his arm over my shoulder kissing my hair. Approaching Coors Field, the lights are bright and you can hear the announcer introducing the teams.

We breeze our way through security and head straight to our seats. I follow behind Abel, holding his hand tightly, and relishing the way it feels to be with him. He leads us closer and closer to the field, finally stopping at the fourth row behind third base. Our seats are amazing; we have a clear view of the entire field. We are seated above the Diamondbacks dugout, so there are a ton of Diamondbacks fans.

The field is basically surrounded by a huge wall of people, so many more than I expected. I didn't think tickets sold very well here, but clearly I was mistaken. That explains the crowds out front and the insane energy. It's also the beginning of the season, and our weather has been rockin'.

"Abel, these seats are amazing. How did you get these tickets?"

Before he answers me, a beer guy comes down the stairs. Abel signals him with his fingers that we'll take two, and takes out his wallet. "From the station. My battalion chief had them and asked if I wanted them."

"Any time he has extra tickets, I'm down to go."

He hands me my beer, and kisses behind my ear. "I plan on taking you to a lot more games."

I lean into him and rest my free hand on his thigh. "I want you bad," I whisper.

He pulls the skin on my neck into his mouth, sucking hard, instantly making me wet. "Remember, we're going to take it slow tonight. Be patient, kitten."

I pull away from him and look into his sexy, hazel eyes. He's still leaning over, his elbow resting on the armrest between our seats. I stick out my bottom lip and do my best to pout. Abel grabs the back of my head, gently pulling me towards him, biting my lip. "Patience, okay?"

I kiss him, then the crowd cheers and everyone stands as the first batter up heads to home plate. We do the same, and I see the Diamondbacks are all scattered across the field and ready to play. I set my beer down to whistle and clap, as some of the other fans cheer behind me. Abel looks at me and shakes his head, taking a swig of his beer.

Todd Helton is up first for the Rockies. He's a good hitter and their first baseman. He has had a ton of home runs in his career and we have to use caution when pitching to him. Sitting back down, I can tell Abel is staring at me as I lean forward, watching intently. My stomach is in knots. As soon as the pitcher throws the ball, it's a strike. He makes this look easy. Another two pitches and he strikes Helton out. Next up for the Rockies is their outfielder. He's a lefty and I know this won't be a problem. One throw and he whacks the ball, popping it high in the air. Our centerfielder waves that he's got it and catches it easily. Next up and hopefully last for the Rockies is their third baseman. Three pitches later, he strikes out. I jump and scream, high-fiving the Diamondbacks fan next to me. I turn to Abel and lean down kissing him, not caring who sees us in that moment of excitement.

"We are so going to annihilate you guys."

He chuckles at me. "Wanna bet on that?"

"Absolutely," I say and sit back down.

"If your team wins, then you can do anything you want to me in bed. But if my team wins, then you're at my mercy."

I immediately reach my hand out and shake his. That's an easy bet; I already told him he can do whatever he wants to me. A sly smile extends across his face. "Don't be so quick to shake. You might regret it later."

I turn my attention back to the game, because I know I won't. For me, it's a win-win. The game progresses at a quick pace, and before I know it, we are at the bottom of the ninth inning. The crowd is all on their feet, as the Rockies try and strike out the Diamondbacks' catcher. The bases are loaded, and there are two outs, and the score is tied. As the Rockies pitch, the Diamondbacks' catcher smacks the ball. The runner on third heads home and slides into base.

I turn to Abel and he has a smug grin on his face. "Why are you smirking at me?" I ask.

"To be honest, I'm excited to see what you have in mind for our bet."

I lean down and whisper in his ear, "You'll have to wait and see."

I'm standing in Abel's bathroom, naked and staring at myself in the mirror. I know we agreed to try and take things slow tonight, but I don't know if I can do that, and I think our bet makes it null and void for tonight. Besides, neither of us has ever had slow sex, but I suppose it wouldn't hurt to try.

Since I'm in charge, I decide to wing things and let what happens happen. As I exit the bathroom, Abel isn't in the bedroom. I walk quietly into the living room and still nothing. I look out onto his patio and there he is. His back is to me and he's leaning over the railing. At that moment it hits me what I want to do, so I turn off all the lights inside his condo and slide the back door open. He turns to me and shakes his head as I stand naked before him. I flip the last light off, the patio light, and now everything is dark. All I can see is his silhouette and the twinkling night sky. He walks towards me and slides his arms around my body, pulling me securely against him.

"Christ, you're sexy. What do you have in mind for tonight?" he asks.

"I thought we could enjoy the view and spend some time outside?"

Just then, I hear the neighbors below us laugh. They must be outside enjoying the night as well. "Are you sure?" he asks.

I walk past him and lean over the railing enjoying the darkness and this amazing view. Abel is behind me, resting his hands on the railing and whispers in my ear, "You're in charge tonight, kitten. Tell me what you want."

I turn around to look at him and can see the reflection of the city lights in his eyes. "I want you naked," I whisper into his ear, aware there are other people out here.

He removes his t-shirt, throwing it to the ground and unzips his pants. I can tell he's looking at me as he steps out of them. He then removes his underwear and walks up to me.

"What else?" he asks, bracing the railing behind me. His body is inches from mine and hot; I can feel the heat radiating off of him in waves.

"I want to take things slow," I say. And that's the truth. I don't have a preference what we do as long as we don't fuck like animals. I want to experience a slow, passionate evening, and I want it to be with Abel.

"If I do anything too fast, just tell me," he says. I nod my head and lean into him. We don't kiss or rush moving our lips to touch one another's. We just stare at each other. The closest we get to touching in this moment is our mingled breathing and my nipples lightly brushing his chest with every breath.

My heart is racing, and finally, when I can take it no longer, I wrap my arms around him, pulling his body against mine. He slowly takes his hands and grabs my face, winding his fingers into my hair. Then he pulls our mouths to touch and kisses me. I dig my nails into his back and remember that tonight is about taking things slow. I remove them and look up into his eyes. He looks at me with a smile and reaches down to grab his cock. He nudges the head against my sex and opens my swollen lips. Once he has me exposed and vulnerable to him, I focus on staying quiet as he rubs my pussy.

Abel sticks to his word and never forces things to move faster. He keeps the same rhythm and I feel a very strong orgasm coming on. I place one of my arms around his neck and grip my breast with the other, squeezing and tantalizing my nipple in between my fingers.

I hold onto my orgasm as Abel stops rubbing the outside of my pussy and sinks deep inside of me. He rests his hands on my hips and looks at me to make sure I'm okay. I move my mouth to his and we begin kissing, slowly, the same way our bodies move. Things are intense, coupled with the fact that we have to be quiet has everything in overdrive. Since Abel is so big, standing and having sex this way is no problem. Every time he moves in and out of me, his dick rubs my clit, which feels amazing. I let go of his arms and reach behind me to brace the railing. I lean back and the position is perfect. Abel makes low moans thrusting his long cock back and forth. His noises stop once his mouth touches my body, kissing and sucking everywhere he can. His hands are riveted tightly on my hips, his fingers are on my back, and his thumbs are resting on the front.

I can't help but whimper as I look up at him. The outline of his body is gorgeous, and the care he is taking with me is like nothing I've ever felt before. He takes his eyes off of my body and locks them with mine. Although it's dark outside I can tell he's looking at me. His moans start again making mine get louder. I hear the people below us laughing. I'm not sure if they can hear us or not, but at this point I really don't care.

I let go and come long and hard. It seems to last forever as Abel's slow movements stroke the inside of my cunt and my clit all at the same time. He doesn't pick up speed even as he comes and pumps himself deep inside of me. As we both calm our breathing and stare at each other, I notice the people downstairs are particularly quiet. Then I hear them go inside, closing their door rather loudly. I laugh and pull myself up to Abel. He does the same as he nudges my neck with his mouth.

"*Now* they go inside," he says and nibbles on my ear lobe.

"I know, right? But wasn't it fun to go slow and be quiet?"

Still sucking my neck as he starts to move his dick in and out of me again, he sighs, "That was the best."

He continues and I become nothing but sensation, every nerve ending firing on pure ecstasy. Hugging him, he grabs my legs and lifts me up. I search for his mouth and kiss him eagerly as he walks us backwards to the outdoor couch. Gently he lowers my body onto the cool fabric, bringing himself down on top of me. As soon as we are pressed together, he begins to move, but not with his normal urgency. We take our time. I slowly move my hips to meet his long, slow thrusts. Instead of kissing him I move my mouth to his neck, kissing and sucking.

In that moment, I'm lost. Lost in Abel and everything that matters. I don't care that we're outside and on his balcony. I don't care that others could hear us or, quite frankly, see us. All I care about is this euphoria. I continue to ravish his neck and as soon as I feel my orgasm come on, I let go. Again, Abel's thrusts are long and slow as he comes with me. I finally remove my lips from his neck and look into his eyes.

"You know that's gonna leave a mark," he says.

A surprised expression uncoils on my face. "I wasn't that rough, was I?"

He nods his head and leans down kissing behind my

ear. "I don't mind though. I actually really, really liked it," he says pressing his lips behind my ear again.

"I'm sure it won't leave a mark," I say as we get up and head inside. Abel collects his clothes and I head into the bathroom. When I come out, he is in bed and Puss is at his feet. He lifts the covers for me and I climb in naked, nestling myself in his arms.

"I'm going to miss you these next three days," he says.

"I know, so am I," I say and leave it at that. Inside of me, I want to get all clingy, but I don't. My typical habits have kicked in and my emotions are on the brink of spiraling out of control. I know a lot of my past heartbreak has been the result of me scaring guys off, and I really don't want to do that with Abel. Hell, I'm determined to not do that with him.

Chapter 9

Three Days

I'm happy to finally be off of work. I've worked three swing shifts and they were brutal. Not to mention I had to cancel my lunch plans with Ben and that was awkward. I went from telling him that Abel was just my friend to then using him as my excuse as to why I couldn't have lunch with him. On a brighter note, Abel convinced me to have dinner with him and the guys at the station. I guess I did promise to make my sub sandwiches, and it's Abel's night to cook. I'm giddy and have butterflies in the pit of my stomach. It's been almost three full days since I've seen him. I know I always fall fast and hard, but with Abel I really am trying to keep my emotions in check. Things feel different, and I hope that's because they are different.

Locking my front door, the sun is warm on my back as I make my way to my car. I decided to wear a pair of denim shorts, a sheer and flowy cream tank, and strappy tweed wedge sandals. One of the things I love about Abel is that it doesn't matter what shoes I wear because of how tall he it. Normally with guys in the past, I've always had to wear flats, but not with Abel.

The station isn't far from my house and when I pull up, all of the guys are out front playing basketball. They are all shirtless, sweaty, and yummy. Abel sees me and shoots the ball — of course scoring — and jogs over to me. As soon as I'm on my feet, he wraps me in his arms, pressing me into the rear door of my car.

His mouth is on mine, and man, he tastes good. Slowly, he moves his hand underneath the thin fabric of my shirt caressing my skin. My whole body ignites instantly and I want to fuck him so bad I would do it right here, right now, and not care who saw us. Before I lose control, I slow the kiss and thread my fingers into his hair.

"Hi," I whisper.

He leans down and kisses behind my ear, "Hey, kitten. Shit, I've missed you."

"You have no idea. As much as I want to stand here and kiss you all day, we can't. I have a meal to cook, and I see a bunch of hungry guys staring at us. Plus my self-control at this moment is paper thin, so back up, buddy," I tease jokingly.

"I hate to say that you're right, but you are. Besides, the guys are so excited to try your subs. I've been talking about them all day." He grabs my hand and we walk over to the group of guys. Most of them I know from the BBQ and they're all really sweet. We exchange friendly hellos and then everyone heads into the station.

On top of the garage that holds their equipment and fire trucks is a large, open, loft-style house. I love the feel in here; it reminds me of Abel's loft with the open floor plan and huge kitchen.

"Do you guys mind if we shower?" Troy asks us.

"Of course not," I say. They all leave and head to the other side of the house. Abel opens the fridge and starts to pull out the ingredients for dinner.

"I bought everything on the list you emailed me and then some. Most of the guys eat like I do, so I wanted to make sure we had plenty of food."

"Thank you," I say and kiss him on the shoulder. "You can go shower if you want to."

He shakes his head saying, "Absolutely not. I've been waiting to see you for three full days; I'm not about to leave you to shower. Plus, it's my night to cook and I want to help you. Tell me what I can do."

"Would you rather wash the veggies or cut them?"

"I'll wash."

I hand him everything that needs to be washed and start looking around for a cutting board and a knife. As I rummage in the last cabinet, I come up with only the knife. Turning to look at Abel to ask him if he knows where the cutting board is, he is staring at my ass. I laugh at him and it immediately pulls him out of his trance.

"I can see that you're preoccupied, but you need to be washing the vegetables," I tease.

He smiles at me and turns the water on. "Sorry, kitten."

"Don't be sorry. I'm just teasing you. Do you know where a cutting board is?"

He pulls it off the top of the fridge and hands it to me.

We go through the process of preparing the subs. We make more than I ever have; I sure hope these guys can eat them all. When we all sit to eat, the guys are bantering back and forth. I love how comfortable Abel is here, joining in with their fun. After dinner, some of the other guys clean up since we cooked, allowing Abel and I to head out to the back deck.

I hate that I have to leave him. I want nothing more than to stay the night together. Looking out on the back view of the city, Abel grabs my hips and kisses me behind my ear.

"Fuck, I've missed you, Cara. I didn't know it would be this hard to be away from you."

I lean my head to the side and Abel rests his chin on my shoulder. His breathing is fast, as is mine, and I wish we could sneak away.

"Will you stay the night at my house and I'll leave here as soon as I can? I need to be with you, inside of your sweet, little cunt as soon as possible."

"Of course I will; I need you too. What time do you

think you'll be off?"

He sucks on my neck and then says, "We switch shifts at 7:00a.m. But I'm going to try and leave here sooner."

I turn around and place my hands on his bare, tattooed chest. "I should get going. We both know that our control isn't very good right now. I'll be waiting for you."

He nods his head and kisses my forehead. I know better than to even begin kissing him. The sexual tension flowing between us is so strong that there is nothing in this world that would stop either one of us.

When we walk back inside, the guys are all lounging around watching a baseball game.

"Thank you for the subs, Cara," Troy says. "They were the bomb," Matt adds.

"You guys are too nice. They're so easy to make. Thanks for having me for dinner," I say, and Abel walks me out handing me the key to his loft. I contemplate driving home and grabbing some of my things, but I really am too tired and I want to rest for two reasons. One, the sooner I sleep, the sooner I see Abel. And two, I need to rest because I know we are going to do nothing but fuck all day tomorrow.

Pulling into his underground garage, I park in one of his assigned spots and walk into the building. My phone chimes with a text. I check and it's Alexa.

Hey, girl, long time no talk. How are you? Do you want to

go shopping or have lunch tomorrow?

I press the call button for the elevator and contemplate what to text her back, since she doesn't know about Abel and I yet. I know that I can't make plans with her for tomorrow, so I lie instead.

I work seven to seven tomorrow, but I'm off after that. Would you and Vincent like to come over and have dinner the following night, I'll cook?

She immediately texts me back, *That's perfect. I'll talk to Vincent and we'll let you know what time.* I think it's time Abel and I tell them about us. I know he won't care, so I'll bring up dinner to him and I think that will be the perfect time to share our news.

Entering Abel's loft, I'm greeted by a very vocal and excited Puss. She must be lonely because she hasn't seen him for the last three days. I set my purse on the counter and pet her. Then I snag a beer from the fridge and notice he has three little bottles of lime juice in there. I can't drink a beer without my lime juice and he knows it. I smile to myself at his sweet gesture and drench my beer full of it. Taking a sip, it's so delicious. I head into Abel's room and pull out a pair of his sweats and one of his Denver Fire t-shirts. I strip, pull his clothes on, and get lost in the scent. God, it smells like him. I contemplate watching TV in his bed, but decide to go to the living room.

Once I'm comfy on the couch, I text Abel to tell him I'm here. My eyes are already heavy and when Puss jumps up, purring for attention, her warmth makes me even sleepier. She lies down at my feet. I flip through the channels and settle on watching a rerun of *Jersey Shore*. Sleep creeps in and I quickly drift off, dreaming of none other than my sexy, tattooed Abel.

I wake to warm hands pulling my sweatpants down. Blinking a few times, I look to see a naked and beautiful Abel standing above me. I moan and lift my hips, looking at his hard and waiting cock. As his hands glide the pants down my legs, it sends a tingle throughout my system. I try hard to keep my eyes open, but I can't.

Once he has me completely naked, his warm lips kiss behind my ear. It's by far my favorite spot, and he knows it. Moving my hands to touch him and pull him on top of me, a low laugh escapes his throat. He doesn't stay lying still for long, as his mouth gets him moving, scattering kisses from my neck down my body. When I look down at him, he's staring at my sex with intense desire. Watching him like this makes me wet. Slowly he dips his tongue into my awaiting pussy, moving it from my clit to my anus and back up. It's fucking electrifying. No one has ever touched me there but Abel, and Christ, I don't want him to stop.

"One day, I'm going to fuck you here," he whispers into my skin.

Unable to get out any coherent words, I mumble, "Mhhhh."

He goes back to work, gliding his tongue up and

down my pussy. Enjoying the feeling far too much, I can't stop myself from grabbing his hair. Once I touch him, he starts flicking and sucking my clit. I fist the fabric of the couch with my other hand, grabbing onto any surface I can grip. I desperately try to hold on, knowing I'm about to come. I'm being greedy and I know it, trying to hold on. It's been three days, and my body has missed him, missed this and what we have. But he's too damn good and I let go, whimpering in pleasure. Abel's hands are a vice on my hips, holding me to him. He starts moving back and forth at a quicker pace as I lose it.

Everything within me trembles as I explode, convulsing with pleasure, loving this feeling that only this man can give me. He slows his movements, and still I want more. I will *never* get enough of him or what we have. I know it's soon, but I don't care.

Abel sits up and I follow, kneeling on the couch before him. He leans back into the corner, and I contemplate whether to fuck him or devour him with my mouth. Looking into his gleaming hazel eyes, I rest my hands on his thighs and kiss behind his ear. I follow the same path he did and leave a trail of kisses down his tattooed body. As I reach his cock, there's a small amount of cum on the tip. I swipe it with my index finger and then suck it off. He watches me with hunger, as I move my finger slowly in and out of my mouth. Damn, he tastes so good. Needing more, I lean in and tightly grip him with my hand. I slide him into my mouth and make it almost all the way down. I keep moving up and down with my lips while matching my movements with my hand.

Abel grabs one of my breasts and pinches my nipple. *Fuck, he knows what I like.* I stop sucking him, and look into his eyes.

"Damn, I love your mouth, Cara."

I smile and hover over him as he moves away from the corner of the couch. Aggressively, he takes my sensitive bud between his teeth, sending a chill from head to toe. I go into a frenzy, reaching between us and sliding down on his rock-hard dick. The pleasure is instant and intense. Abel continues to torment my breasts, while I move up and down. I try to take my time and go slow. I want to savor this time with him, every time with him, but I can't. He has my body searching for pleasure, a pleasure I have never known until now.

Tightening my pussy around him I tip my head back, I'm moving too fast for him to concentrate on my breasts any longer. His strong hands possessively grip my hips, slamming me onto him. My body shudders as I feel an orgasm building. Before I can let go, Abel flips us over. I'm now pinned below him, panting and pissed that he stopped.

"Cara, you were about to unman me in all of thirty seconds. I've missed your pink, little pussy, and I don't want this to end. Let me take my time. I want to fuck you so slowly that your body won't be able to stop from convulsing with pleasure. You know how good we are together when we take our time." He begins to move, making long slow stokes. "Now touch your clit. But *don't* make yourself come. Got it?"

I nod my head and immediately start to touch myself. There is no other man in the world that could get me to do things like this. He moans softly with each thrust as he pulls himself out of me and then glides back in. I move my fingers quickly and have to force myself to stop, as I'm about to come. I grip his forearms and look down at our bodies as they move together.

We are both looking down at my pink, swollen pussy as I devour him. Watching us is too much, and I can't stop the waves of pleasure as they take over my body. I moan in elation letting go. Abel picks up speed, moving his hard cock with precision and throws his head back as he comes. I'm still bracing his forearms as I watch him pump himself inside of me. The veins in his neck are straining and every muscle in his body is flexing. Slowing his movements, he leans down, lying on top of me.

Gently, I trace his back with my fingers, feeling his warm breath on my skin. I love how our bodies react and work together. He gently nuzzles my neck like he can't get close enough, and we both drift off to sleep.

Chapter 10

Surprise

"Baby, will you please stop so I can cook breakfast?" I can barely get the words out. Abel currently has me pinned against the refrigerator.

"I told you I don't want food, kitten."

I laugh at him and quickly stop when his strong hand firmly grips my ass. He kisses my neck and is interrupted by a knock on the front door. *Thankfully, because I'm starving.* He swats my bare ass, and walks to the front door. I go back to the fridge, this time opening it and removing the eggs. As soon as the door opens I hear a familiar voice and freeze. I look to my left and standing there are Alexa and Vincent. I'm scared shitless to be standing before them in just Abel's t-shirt.

Looking into Alexa's eyes, I can see she is pissed. "You have got to be kidding me," she snaps.

Before I can say anything she turns on her heel and walks out. I rush to the door and yell out after her, "Wait,

Lex! Just let us explain."

She throws her hands up in the air and is out of sight as she rounds the corner. As horrible as I feel, I can't run after her in just a t-shirt. I turn around to see the guys both talking in low tones. As they see me, I say, "Vince, I'm sorry we haven't told you guys. I planned on it at dinner tomorrow night."

He looks at me like an older brother would. "Don't be sorry. I can't say I'm surprised. I saw this coming and I'm sure Alexa did too. She's probably just upset she didn't know. I'll talk to her. Let's still plan on dinner so you two can talk, and so I can grill this douchebag and make sure he's good enough for you."

Abel punches his arm saying, "Hey, whose side are you on?"

"I'm sorry, bro, but Cara's like a sister to me. And your track record with women is less than stellar. I know you've wanted things to work out with her for a while, but I have concerns, that's all."

"Fine. You can grill me all you want. I'm not going to hurt her."

"Good," Vincent says pulling us both into a hug. As he kisses the top of my head, I look at Abel and he winks at me. "Why don't you guys come to our house tomorrow at six?"

I nod my head and Vincent leaves. I immediately look at Abel as he closes the door. He can read the anxiety on my face and wraps me in his warm arms. I hug him back and nestle my cheek on his chest.

"Abel, maybe us doing this is a bad idea."

He pulls away from me and grabs my face. "This is not a bad idea. Don't say that."

I nod my head and walk away. I need to take a few moments to myself. Escaping to the balcony is the only place I can go. I know I want to be with Abel, but my own insecurities are now creeping in, seeing Alexa react the way she did.

Fuck, why did I lie to her?

She's my closest friend besides my sister, and I should've been honest with her from the beginning. Instead I've been lying to her for months about my feelings. I told her I wasn't interested in being with Abel, when all along I was wrestling with the fact that I *did* want him. He is all I thought about for months and completely consumed my mind. I knew being with him came with a risk and I fought it hard. I've done this so many times, allowing guys to get in the way of my logical thinking. I was so swept up in him and what we have to even care about how my actions might affect those closest to me.

Before I can mind fuck myself any longer, Abel is behind me. He wraps his arms around my body and holds me tightly. He gently kisses behind my ear and turns me around to face him. When he looks into my red eyes he shakes his head and says, "Don't cry, kitten. I get that you're upset, but Alexa will get over this. Whatever you do, please don't question what's going on between us. I know for me, I've never felt anything more right." He wipes a tear off of my cheek with his thumb. I rarely cry, and when I do it's always alone, but Alexa is just so important to me that I can't keep my emotions in check. My stomach is clenched in a ball of knots and I just want to make things right with her.

"Trust me, Abel, when I look at you, I don't question what we have at all. But seeing Alexa react the way she did absolutely kills me. Not only did she not know about us at all, but I outright lied to her. I told her I had to work today when she called me last night."

"Just give her a little space. I'm sure she's not mad to know we're dating, more so the fact you lied to her. Put yourself in her shoes."

"I hope she'll be happy for us. But deep down I'm worried that she is going to be a hard ass on us. I acted that way with her and Vincent. Things between the three of us were awkward for a while."

"Would you feel better if you called her? You can't start stressing about things you don't know yet."

Nodding my head at him, Abel goes inside to grab my phone. He's right — I need to talk to her before I start overreacting. He comes outside and hands me my phone. Immediately I call her, and it rings once and goes to voicemail. I can tell she purposely declined my call.

Once Abel goes back inside, I dial again. I feel desperate about making things right with her. This time it rings half a ring and goes straight to voicemail. Walking over to the couch, I feel defeated as I curl up into the soft fabric. I close my eyes and sulk, unable to enjoy the beautiful city view.

Abel comes outside, pulling my mind away from the guilt that is eating me up. He has two cups of coffee in his hands and looks hot as hell.

Handing me the coffee, he says, "I was going to make breakfast, but I wanted to make you feel better, not worse."

"You don't need to cook. I've lost my appetite anyways," I say, taking a long sip of the hot deliciousness he just handed me.

"Can we do something today to keep your mind off of Alexa?"

"It depends what you have in mind," I say with a serious expression.

"Do you trust me?"

"Of course I trust you. But that doesn't answer my question."

"I didn't answer your question on purpose. I want you to focus on the element of surprise. Can you do that?" he says, sweeping my hair off of my shoulder and kissing my neck.

I nod my head and a small moan escapes my throat.

"Don't start with that, kitten, or we'll never get out of here and to your surprise."

I smile at him and move to straddle his lap.

Wrapping my arms around his neck, I feel that familiar ache between my legs. Leaning down, I kiss him and he doesn't hesitate a second kissing me back. I open my mouth and his tongue invades, exploring and teasing, making me want him even more. When I moan again, Abel stands. I keep my grip tight on his neck and lock my feet behind his back. He doesn't stop kissing me as he walks into the house with a clear purpose. His hands clench my thighs and dig into my skin.

When we enter his bedroom, I unhook my legs and stand before him on my own two feet. Slowly, Abel stops kissing me and looks into my eyes. Resting his forehead on mine he asks, "Do you want your surprise or not?"

I playfully slap his arm. "Of course I want my surprise."

"Well, you're making it really hard for me to think of anything else besides your wet, little cunt."

"She'll be with you all day and can wait for you tonight, or you can please her now. She's throbbing for you, if you want her."

"Trust me, Cara, I want her," he says.

Tilting my head to the side, I wrap my hands around his neck and tug him to me. Not wasting a moment, he kisses me back as we fall on the bed and I bind my legs around him again. His dick is pulsating, hard, and ready for me. Hovering his body over mine, he rests the head of his cock against me.

Moving one of my hands, I trace up and down his

back. Slowly moving, he grinds himself against me. Jesus, I'm wet and the slickness allows him to glide up and down. He continues to do this until he spreads my legs wide and slides inside of me, inch by inch, looking in my eyes. Grabbing both of my hands, he pins them above my head and begins to move. My mouth goes into a frenzy leaving kisses all over him. Every bit of his skin I can touch, I kiss. Keeping his movements slow and steady, he works us both. Yes, he might have my hands pinned with his, but this is what I like. I love to submit to him and let him do with me as he pleases.

I flex my pussy and he moans loudly, slowing down. Taking his free hand he traces my lips with one of his fingers and says, "Don't do that, or I'll come."

Breathlessly I say, "I want you to come."

"I know. So do I, but not yet."

Releasing the grip I have on his cock, he begins to move again, finally letting go of my hands. He grabs my breasts as they move with us. My pink nipples are hard, and when he flicks his tongue over one, my entire breast tightens.

"Please, make us come," I whisper.

Experiencing the pleasure he pulls out of my body to the fullest, I tighten my core again and it pushes him over the edge. Grunting, he pulls almost all his length out of me and moves back in, repeating this over and over as he releases, coming inside of me. His movements hit the right spot for me as I dig my fingernails into his skin and cry out his name.

Watching us come together like this has to be the sexiest thing I've ever seen. Looking at me through heavy lids, he rolls off of me and I hop up.

"Fuck, that was good. But now we have to hurry, so get dressed," he says and slaps my ass.

I squeal and do as I'm told. As I dress, I can't keep my eyes off of him, although my mind is still elsewhere. I watch intently as he puts on a pair of dark jeans with a black v-neck t-shirt and black tennis shoes. Finally I stop staring and go outside to grab my phone and bring our coffee cups in. As I pour them into to-go mugs, I'm startled as my phone buzzes. When I look at it, it's my sister texting me.

Don't forget about nana's birthday next month. Have you decided if you're going to drive or fly?

I won't forget and I haven't decided what I want to do. I'll let you know.

Okay, let me know. Love you.

"Who's that?" Abel says, grabbing two bottles of water from the fridge.

"It's my sister. Next month is my grandma's birthday. So I have to go home and she asked if I was going to drive or fly."

"Have you decided?"

"I don't know. I haven't thought a lot about it."

"Well, if you need help deciding I'm here for you. Are you ready to get going?"

I nod my head and we leave the loft. Now on top of worrying about Alexa, I can't help but think about my impending trip back home. My father passed away during my senior year of college in a plane crash. It was always a dream of his to fly his own plane, and he was actually learning to become a pilot when it happened. I haven't flown since then. I always drive when I go home to Arizona, even though it's a brutal twelve hours by myself.

When the elevator opens, Abel moves quickly to his truck, helping me in and handing me the waters. As he walks around to climb into his side of the huge Ford Raptor, I rest my head against the leather headrest.

"I can tell you're still stressing."

I roll my head to the side and look at his stunning profile as he backs the truck out. "I'm sorry. I don't want to be stressed today, but I can't help it."

"Is it just Alexa?"

"That and now the trip next month."

He rests his hand on my knee and pulls onto the highway. "Alexa will get over this; just give her a little bit of time. Why are you stressed about next month?"

"I don't want to bother you with my issues. I'll figure it out."

"You're not bothering me. I asked because I want to know. Tell me."

"My dad passed away in a plane crash a few years back and I haven't been able to bring myself to fly since then. Now when I go home I drive, but it's twelve hours and sucks by myself."

Abel doesn't say anything to my statement and I can tell that he is processing what I just told him. "I'm sorry, kitten. I knew he had passed, I just didn't know how. When exactly are you going?"

"It's okay. I'll be gone Memorial Day weekend."

"Would it help if I went with you?"

I never thought to ask him to come with me or imagined that he would want to. "Would you want to?"

"I'm asking, aren't I?"

"Yeah, it would help. But I don't want you to have to spend the weekend away from home, and umm, my mom ... well, she's a little over the top."

"I want to go if you'll let me, and trust me, I can handle your mom."

"Thank you," I say, squeezing his hand.

Pulling the truck into a parking spot he turns towards me. "Cara, you don't need to thank me. I want to do this; that's what boyfriends do."

That comment takes my breath away. I can't believe he just said that to me. Excitement takes over and I wrap my arms around his neck. He hugs me back and I kiss him hard on the lips.

Pulling away he says, "Well, I'm glad to see that made you feel better."

Nodding my head I kiss him again.

"Good, because now it's time for your surprise."

"I can't wait! I love surprises."

We both climb out of the truck and I notice my feet hit soft gravel as I land on the ground. Abel grabs my hand as we start walking up a dirt hill. "Are you scared of heights?" he asks.

"No. Why? Are we hiking up a mountain?"

He looks at my feet in my strappy sandals and laughs. "In those shoes? No, we're not doing any hiking today."

I glare at him and say, "Hey, what is it with you and my shoes?"

"Nothing. In fact, I would love to see you in nothing but those shoes later. But you always seem to wear the wrong shoes for the occasion."

Once we reach the top of the hill, I'm unable to process what is before me. It's a huge cement bridge with two people standing in the center of it. Then they are gone. Holy shit, they just jumped!

I look at Abel as excitement races through me. I've always wanted to bungee jump and he is going to make that happen today. I squeeze his hand and then let go. Running off, I can't wait to get to the edge and see how long the fall is.

Looking down at the couple that just jumped, they are wrapped around each other and laughing. The line that is strapped to their feet holds a small amount of tension as it keeps them bobbing up and down. The ground has to be at least two hundred feet away.

Abel is beside me and wraps his arm around my

waist. I can't take my eyes off of the couple that is still hanging upside down. I feel him watching me as he kisses behind my ear. When I look over at him I can tell he is just as excited.

"So you're okay with this?" he asks.

"Oh my God, yes. I've always wanted to do this. It's on my bucket list for sure."

"Good, so have I. I'm happy I get to do it with you."

"Me too," I say and kiss him.

Our arms are wrapped around each other as we walk up to a makeshift storefront made out of an old, silver camper. Behind the counter is a young surfer looking chick, with long blonde hair and a freckled face.

"How can I help you guys?" she asks.

"We have a reservation to jump at noon today," Abel says.

"What's the last name?"

"Mileski."

"Abel and Cara?"

"Yup, that's us."

"Here's some paperwork I need you to fill out; please read it carefully. Then head around back and Chad will help you from there."

I skim over the document. It's the standard we-are-not-responsible-if-you-die and other legal mumbo jumbo. If you're going to do this, then there's obviously risk and I know that, so I sign. Turning around, I watch another couple as they are being instructed at the bridge.

"Aren't you going to read that?" Abel asks.

"I did."

He shakes his head and chuckles at me while signing his contract and then pays the girl. As we round the corner, Chad stands to greet us. He has a huge smile like a Cheshire cat and crystal blue eyes.

"Hey, guys, I'm Chad. I'll be helping you today."

"Hey, man, I'm Abel and this Cara," Abel says shaking Chad's hand.

I shake his hand as well. "It's nice to meet you," I say.

Chad directs us to have a seat in two chairs and goes over all of the instructions. He is patient, which I like, but at the same time I'm extremely antsy to get going. Within ten minutes we are walking over to the bridge. I grab Abel's hand, squeezing it tightly, and notice it's sweaty. When I look up into his eyes, he looks nervous.

"You okay?" I ask, giving his hand a gentle squeeze for reassurance.

He nods his head, but doesn't speak. As we reach the bridge, Chad and another guy strap up our ankles ensuring that all of the safety procedures have been followed. My heart is starting to race as pure adrenaline flows through me. I can't believe I'm about to jump off a bridge. When Abel and I face each other, I want to take his worry away. I grab his face and pull his lips to mine, completely oblivious to our surroundings as I deepen the kiss. In this moment we could be surrounded by dozens of people or completely alone, all I know is that I'm without a care in the world.

When I pull away, a small smile creeps across his face.

"Better?" I ask.

"Much better."

Chad interrupts our moment, "Alright, you two. You'll have plenty of time to kiss at the bottom. You're free to fall whenever you like."

Wrapping my arms tightly around Abel's waist I squeeze and lock my fingers behind his back. He does the same to me and asks, "Are you ready, baby?"

I am, so I try to lean, but I'm too small to move us both. Abel gives me a smug look and easily sends us plummeting over the edge. My chin digs into his chest and I grip his body even more as we fly towards the ground. Falling gives me the feeling I remember as a child, a stomach full of butterflies racing maniacally, and I can't help but giggle excitedly. All of the blood rushes to my head and right as it seems we are going to crash into the ground, the tension from the rope yanks us back up. I'm absolutely dizzy with giddiness as we cling to each other upside-down, and all I can think is this has got to be the best roller coaster ride ever! We continue bouncing up and down, but less with each bob. Who knew the power of gravity could be this amazing!

As we slow, Abel moves his hand, grabbing the back

of my neck. He puts his mouth on the skin of my shoulder, kissing and sucking. *He's such a tease.* I pull away from his chest and before I can get a good look at him, he invades my mouth. His kiss is all dominating as we tangle tongues, the rush from the fall fueling our passion. This whole experience feels like something out of a fairy tale; being with Abel is my fairy tale. His muscles are hard and tense under my grip, and as much as I want to move my hands to explore his body, I don't. I'm too lost in this moment, in this kiss, and in this man.

Chapter II

Alexa

Alexa hasn't answered or responded to any of my calls or text messages. Now I'm a nervous fucking wreck, as we are about to go to her and Vincent's house for dinner.

"Baby, you look fine. Will you stop changing? Alexa's not going to care what you're wearing."

I have to admit that Abel is right as I look at myself in the mirror. I'm wearing a long, dark pink, cotton skirt with a white tank top. I decide to stick with the outfit and slip on a pair of brown leather flip flops and my short jean jacket.

I turn and look at Abel. He is lounging on my bed, lying against my headboard in gray jeans, a white t-shirt, and a black hoodie. He has the hood pulled up over his baseball hat, and fuck, I think he looks the hottest I've ever seen him.

"Why are you looking at me like that?" he asks, cocking his head.

"I'm just admiring the view."

Standing up, he walks over to me and wraps his arms around my waist. "I could say the same thing. Cara, you're so fucking hot."

He presses his erection against my body, and damn it, I want him. I look at the clock and we are surprisingly running early. Walking us backwards I fumble with the zipper of his pants. Once he reaches my bed, I pull his pants down exposing his hard cock and push his body backwards.

Climbing up next to him, I let my flip flops fall to the floor and start sucking him up and down. He moves his arm, draping it over my body holding me. I love the way he tastes and how he is always ready for me. I keep kneeling and move my hair over to one shoulder.

Pulling away, I grab his dick and jerk him while I look over at his body sprawled out under my ministrations. Abel pulls me to kiss him and I do so, but I never stop stroking his beautiful cock. As our mouths work together, I have to stop kissing him before I give in to temptation, because I'm desperate to lift my skirt up and slide him inside of me.

"You're so beautiful," he says.

"I could say the same thing about you." I get back to work sucking him, clearly enticing him as he thrusts his hips in and out of my mouth. A deep noise builds from within him, driving me to move even faster until he comes in my mouth. I love the feeling when the warm sensation rolls down my throat. But my movements are cut short when Abel pulls away.

"Damn, baby. I can't handle any more of your sweet mouth."

"Good," I say and kiss his neck, hopping off of the bed. I reach for his hand, and he quickly tucks himself back into his pants and zips up before grabbing onto me.

"Are you feeling okay about tonight?" Abel asks as we walk out of my room heading downstairs.

"I don't know. I guess I feel as good as I can. Clearly Alexa is pissed and I don't know how she is going to react tonight."

We load up in Abel's truck and as we pull away from my house he says, "I talked to Vince. She is more hurt that you lied to her than anything else. No matter what happens I'll be right there with you and we'll make it through this. Okay?"

Crossing my arms over my body, I rest my head back and close my eyes. I keep them shut until I feel Abel's hand on my cheek. "You hear me? It's going to be alright, kitten."

I nod my head and focus on deep breaths as we drive across town to Vincent and Alexa's. As we pull into their neighborhood, my phone chimes and I check it. It's a text from Bridgette.

I talked to Lex, she told me about you and Abel. I want you to know how happy I am for the two of you.

Thanks for saying that. I wish Alexa felt the same.

She will, just give her a little time.

"That was Bridgette; she said she's happy for us."

"See, baby? It's going to be fine."

I sure hope so. My stomach is telling me otherwise as it's a ball of nerves as we walk up the front path to their house. Abel rings the doorbell and kisses me on the side of my mouth. Vincent opens it dressed in black dress slacks and a dark purple shirt with the sleeves rolled up and top buttons undone. He has the biggest smile on his face as he hugs me.

I hold back the tears and can't help but laugh when Abel says, "Dude, get your hands off my girl."

Vincent slaps him on the shoulder and looks into my eyes. "Lex is out back. We'll give you both some time alone."

I nod my head and start to walk off, but not before Abel grabs my arm and pulls me back, kissing behind my ear. He doesn't say a word, just that kiss, and lets go of me. I look at him and smile, and then I'm on my way.

I take a deep breath and turn the door handle. Alexa is sitting at the edge of the pool with her feet dangling in the water. She turns and looks at me as I close the door. I smile and she does the same.

"Hey, Lex," I say removing my shoes, sitting next to her and dipping my feet in the water.

"Hey."

I don't know what else to say. I know I can't fuck this up and lose my best friend, not right now. I remember back to a little something my dad taught me when I was little. He always said to make my mom happy he would make a joke.

"Is that your phone in the bottom of the pool?"

She looks at me with wide eyes. "What? Where?"

"I'm just joking. I figured since you've been ignoring me that maybe you lost your phone in the pool."

"Jesus, you're such a snot. No, I didn't lose my phone in the pool. I'm pissed at you and I've been ignoring your incessant messages."

"If I weren't here right now, were you ever going to talk to me?"

She shrugs her shoulders.

"Come on, Lex. I'm sorry I lied to you about working, but I feel like you're overreacting."

"Don't turn this around on me. You not only lied about work, but you and Abel are dating and I was clueless. I'm supposed to be your best friend. Why wouldn't you tell me something like that?"

"I was going to, I promise. We just got so wrapped up in each other, that I pushed all reality aside. And honestly, I was worried about your reaction. I know that sounds immature, but I finally have what I've always wanted and I didn't want to hear any possible objections." She doesn't speak and stares into the water. "Say something, Lex."

"Cara, you know your track record with dating and I'm worried. Neither of you has a good history in that department."

I rub the back of my neck trying to calm myself down. "So what? We are both a little broken. Who's not? You and Vince were not any better when the two of you started dating. Abel has been wonderful, and I really couldn't be any happier. I'm sorry that we didn't tell you, but I can't help how I feel. All I'm asking is that you'll forgive me and support us."

As she grabs my hand, I look over and see tears shining in her eyes. I turn and hug her as tight as I can. "I forgive you, hun. But if that little prick steps out of line, even one time, he's not only going to have me to answer to, but Vincent as well."

"I know. Let's hope he doesn't."

Our hug is interrupted by the guys as they head out back. Each of them has a drink in hand and they are both sexy as fuck. "I'm glad to see you two hugging," Vincent says and reaches for Alexa's hand. She takes it, standing and kissing him like they haven't seen each other all day.

Standing up, I grab a handful of my skirt to keep it off of my wet legs. Abel sets my drink down and goes over to the bench of towels, grabbing me one. On his way back, I can't help the feelings that brew inside of me. He has taken his hoodie off and his thin white t-shirt reminds me of our first night together.

He hands me the towel and I dry my legs, letting my

skirt fall, and take the drink he brought me. I lean up and give him a soft, quick peck. As I pull away, he asks, "Are you okay?"

"Yeah, I am. Thank you for asking."

"Are you guys ready to eat?" Vincent asks.

We all confirm and head inside. Before Abel and I walk through the door, he stops me and grabs my face with one hand and pulls me against him with his other arm. I stare into his gaze and see a side of him I've never witnessed. "Cara, you know that I'll never do anything to hurt you, right?"

"Of course. Why would you even say that?"

"Vincent grilled me and it made me nervous. I want you to know that I have nothing but the best intentions for us and our future."

"I know you do. Don't stress, baby. Okay?" I kiss him on the side of his neck, and he leans into me. We both walk inside and sit at the table with Alexa and Vincent.

Vincent, as usual, prepared a full on feast. He made lasagna, meatballs, garlic bread, and salad. We all fill our plates at the table and pass the serving dishes around.

"So how long have you two been together?" Alexa asks.

I look to Abel and shrug my shoulders. "A few weeks," he responds.

"Frankly, Abel, why should I trust that you aren't going to hurt Cara? Your history with women sucks and she deserves better than that."

I look to Vince and he smiles. Now all of our eyes are on Abel. He swallows hard and takes a sip of his drink. "I have feelings for Cara like I never have for anyone else before. She makes me want to be a better person. She motivates me, she challenges me, and she drives me crazy all at the same time. I can't think about anyone else but her, and just given that one fact, things are already different. I think about my actions and how things will affect her. Our relationship means a lot to me. Trust me, Alexa I know how much she means to you. She means just as much — if not more — to me. You're going to have to give me a chance to prove my intentions."

I'm shocked by his words. Abel has never expressed any of this to me. My mind is racing through what he has just said when my thoughts are interrupted by Alexa.

"Fair enough," she quips back.

"Let's toast to Cara and Abel," Vincent says.

We all raise our glasses and clink them together. I take a long drink of the cool wine, and as soon as I swallow, Abel crushes his warm lips to mine and I melt into him. I don't know if it's the alcohol or his words, but I feel like I can't get enough of him. Just as I'm about to crawl onto his lap, we're cut off.

"Get a fucking room," Vincent growls.

I can't stop myself from going into a fit of giggles. I remember when Abel used to say that to him and Alexa.

"We will. We're gonna get going, but thank you both for dinner and for understanding us."

"Just remember what we talked about."

"I fucking heard you, dude."

"Alright, alright. Now take this lovely young lady home and take care of her, okay?"

We all stand and I notice that everyone is smiling. As hard as Vincent and Abel are on each other, they really do love one another. Looking all around us, I'm overwhelmed by the happiness that fills me knowing that Alexa and Vincent finally know we are dating. More importantly, they accept it and support us. Maybe two black sheep who've made terrible relationship choices in the past can be perfect for each other.

Chapter 12

Mesh

It's been a few weeks since dinner with Alexa and Vincent and things have been great. We all hang out often and have had a blast. I love laughing with Alexa and have missed having so much girl time together. I slam my front door and jog to my car; I'm late for my nail appointment with Alexa, we are meeting for pedicures and I really need to talk to her.

It's getting warmer and warmer every day; today is just bloody hot. Since it's Sunday the traffic is light and I arrive less than 10 minutes late. Walking into the nail salon, I see Alexa lounged back in one of the black, leather massage chairs. When the door chimes announcing my arrival, she instantly smiles, waving me over.

"Hey, honey, sorry I'm late," I say, sliding my shoes off. I pull up my capris and get into the chair next to Alexa.

"Don't be sorry. I was enjoying a moment of Zen."

"Since when do you do any Zen?"

"Since Vincent and I have been taking yoga classes. I've learned a lot of breathing techniques and ways to calm myself. I love it."

"No shit. I couldn't imagine Vincent trying to do yoga. He's like eight feet tall."

I laugh and so does Alexa. Sandy and Vi, our usual nail technicians, come over and get to work on our feet.

"So what's new?" Alexa asks.

"Funny you should ask. Abel's birthday is next week and I want to do something really special for him."

"Why did I not know about this?"

"Ask Vincent," I say, shrugging my shoulders.

She laughs at me and says, "Okay. Abel's birthday is next week. What do you have in mind?"

"Oh God, I'm so nervous. Nothing specific yet, but I want to blow him away. Things are amazing in the S-E-X department and I want to spice it up a bit."

"You have to tell me the details. Is he hung like Vince?"

I giggle and nod my head.

"I knew it. We should go to the sex shop. They have really great gifts. We could get you an outfit and explore all the other stuff. Come on, we have to, my mind is already running with ideas."

"Come on, Lex, don't you have any other ideas?"

"Vince and I have been going lately and they're

awesome. There's a great place we go to across town. The girls that work there are super cool. Wanna go today?"

I'm unsure about doing this. I've never been to a place like that or had experience with anything they have to offer. I know I want to do something different for Abel.

"So are we going or not?" Alexa interrupts my thoughts.

"I don't know … can't we just plan a surprise party or something?"

"Would you really rather hang out with Abel and his friends than be sexy for him and experiment with some kinky stuff?"

"Maybe it wouldn't be that bad."

"Just come check this place out. You don't have to buy anything you don't want to."

I look at Alexa and she is batting her long eyelashes at me. She knows I can never turn her down when she does that.

"Okay, I'll go. But if I don't like anything or the place creeps me out, we're leaving."

She claps her hands and I roll my eyes, resting my head back and enjoying the pedicure. Man, this feels so good. I look down at Vi as she works away. "Do you want black polish?" she asks.

"Yes, please." She knows what I like and I'm a creature of habit. There are some things I just love and can't bear to change and my black toe nail polish is one of them. I look at Lex and she is texting on her phone with a big, corny smile on her face. That reminds me to check mine, and I have two missed texts from Abel.

I don't know how much longer I can sit here waiting for you.

The next says, *Fuck, now my dick's hard thinking about your ass in those pants you're wearing today.*

God, I love him. Holy shit, did I just say that? I've been so good avoiding being all psycho clingy! I can't feel that way, not yet anyways. Pushing that thought aside, I text him back.

As much as I want to handle your dick for you, I can't. Alexa and I are working on top-secret birthday stuff for you, mister.

Okay, I guess I'll manage. I already have blue balls. What time should I meet you at your place?

It's a little after noon now. I figure if Lex and I go to this place and then grab a bite to eat we should be a few hours max.

How about 4:00?

That works for me. Have fun, kitten.

I look at Lex and she has a smirk on her face. "What?" I ask.

"Nothing, I just love to see you smile. I know I was skeptical of Abel in the beginning. But I want you to know how truly happy I am for the two of you."

"Thanks, Lex. I've never been happier."

"I can tell. Is he still going home with you for your grandma's birthday?"

I cringe thinking about my mother. "Yeah. I don't know how it will go over, but we're going next weekend."

"I'm sure it'll be okay. Did you tell Abel about your mom?"

"All I told him was that she is a little overbearing."

Alexa laughs out loud, "Just prepare him for her OCD before you guys get there."

"Okay, you girls are all done," Vi says, as she and Sandy both start to clean up from our pedicures.

I hand Vi my card to pay, "I'll pay for hers as well." Alexa glares at me. "Stop being a snot; you paid last time."

"Fine," she quips at me. "Do you want to follow me to the sex shop?"

"Sure," I say signing the receipt for Vi. I collect my shoes and head for the door, wearing the paper-thin flip-flops the nail salon provides.

"Meet ya there, sweetie," Lex yells from across the parking lot.

I waddle to my car and slide in, following Lex out of the parking lot. The drive across town is quick. The place is brand new and doesn't look at all like what I imagined. Once I have my car in park, I take a moment and put my shoes on. Lex comes strolling over, talking on her cell phone, waiting for me at the front of my car as I finish.

"Do you want the clear or the blue one?" she asks, as I walk up. I'm assuming to Vincent.

When she hangs up and we head inside I ask, "Clear or blue what?"

"Cock ring," she says back.

I can tell by the look on her face she's dead serious.

"Hi, welcome, ladies," a cute sandy blonde says.

"Hi," we both say back and start to look at the amazing selection of items in front of us.

"Oh my fuck, I don't even know where to start," I say.

Alexa looks at me dead in the face, being as serious as she can. "It's a lot to take in, I totally get that. Just look around and think about what you and Abel may like."

I nod my head and follow Alexa around as she shows me the different dildos, lubes, whips, handcuffs, and now cock rings.

"So have you used one of these?" I ask.

"Yeah. They're my new favorite. Our last one just broke, that's why I was asking Vince which one he wanted."

"What exactly is it?"

"It has two functions. They slide down the shaft and are worn at the base. This part," she points to a one-inch bar with different rubber nubs on it, "vibrates. I'm sure you're wondering how they fit being as small as they are compared to our guys. The tightness is an added bonus and causes the cock to become extremely hard — like bone hard."

"Okay, I get it. I'll take one of whichever one you're getting."

"Good. Now let's pick you out an outfit and I think you're all set."

Turning to look at the other side of the store, I know we are going to be a while longer. The other half of the store is the size of a department store, with just as much clothing, although these clothes are in plastic packages like the ones Halloween costumes come in. Lex holds up two packages with scraps of fabric in them and I just shake my head.

As I stand and stare at myself in the mirror, I could absolutely kill Alexa for making me buy this crap. I'm wearing a full on red fishnet outfit and I look like a fucking whore. I knew I should've gone for the naughty nurse's outfit. I guess the only good thing is that it's crotchless.

Sitting on the edge of my bed, I grab my phone to text that little slut and my doorbell rings. Checking the clock it's only 3:45. I grab my robe and jog downstairs. Looking out the peephole, it's Abel. His hair is all combed and looks like he is fresh out of the shower. I open the door and he instantly moves inside taking me in his arms and closes the door behind us. Adrenaline courses through my body as he presses into me.

I move my tongue exploring his mouth and I want to touch him. As I move my hands he stops me, grabbing them and pinning them down next to me. I am helpless beneath his hold. My hands are pinned and my lower body is being held in place by his hips. His ever so present erection shows me how much he really has missed me.

I start to panic because I don't want him to see me in this ridiculous outfit. Stopping the kiss, he rests his forehead against mine. "What's wrong?" he asks.

"Nothing. Trust me, nothing. I just need to change."

Before another moment passes, Abel tears my robe open and stares at my red fishnet-clad body. His breathing stops as his eyes roam over me. "I don't think you need to change at all. In fact, I'm going to demand that this is all that you wear from now on!"

Locking eyes with him, I say, "Really? I thought I looked like a whore."

His hand cups my sex and his fingers quickly discover that this outfit is open. "Cara, you could never look like a whore. Sexy as fuck is how I would describe you."

His skilled fingers separate the edge of my pussy and rub on the inside. Clamping my eyes shut, my head falls against the door as I cry out in desire. Abel's mouth is back on mine as he slides my robe all of the way off.

"Why are you wearing this?" he asks as he picks me

up and starts to walk us upstairs.

I wrap my arms and legs around his body as we move. "It's for your birthday, or it was supposed to be."

"Well, happy early birthday to me."

He lowers us both down onto my bed and I unwrap my legs letting them fall open. Leaning up on his knees, Abel rips his shirt off tossing it to the ground.

When he comes back to me his mouth clamps around one of my hard, exposed nipples. As he's licking and sucking, I reach for his jeans, fumbling to unzip them and get to his hard cock.

"Did you miss my cock, Cara?"

"Mmm-hmm."

"Do you want me to fuck you?"

"Yes, please."

He stands again removing his pants and my legs both fall to one side. "Stay like that," he demands.

I do so and look up at him as he strokes himself until a little cum drips out of the end. With both of my legs to my left, Abel stays standing and nudges the head of his wet cock into me, moving slowly back and forth before he sinks all the way inside of me. "Fuck, I love your ass at this angle, and that I can still see your whole body."

I reach my hands above my head and completely let go, turning over all control as Abel moves inside of me. His movements are slow and deliberate. With each pull and push my body is on the verge of shuddering. Looking up at him, I can see that he is watching himself as he slowly moves in and out of me.

His brows are creased, as if he is in pain from feeling so good. In the next moment he slaps my ass and slaps it hard. I whimper from the pleasure that shoots through me. And then he moves my body so I am bent over for him. My ass is exposed and raised in the air. He starts massaging it, matching our movements.

He brushes his thumb over my anus and says, "God, I want to fuck you so badly here."

Surprisingly, the feeling of him touching me there sets me on fire, and the moment he pushes his thumb inside my body I let go. I have no control and didn't see it coming. I rise up on my hands and push back into him slamming as hard as I can. With his free hand he grabs my hip, digging into my skin and moves me even harder as he lets go. His noises are long and low and sexy as fuck. I look back at him as he comes inside of me. The veins in his neck are protruding and his eyes are shut tight.

He opens them, slowing his movements and smiles at me. I realize then as he removes his thumb that it was still inside me. Apparently I liked how it felt, because I didn't even realize it was there. My body pleads with me to relax after having every muscle constrained, so I lay flat on my stomach and Abel follows. His body is heavy and warm. The only coolness I can feel is from the metal of his nipple piercings pressing into my back. He moves my hair out of his way and starts kissing me, delicately leaving a trail with his lips from my ear down my shoulder and across my back. Then he presses his cheek into my skin and takes a deep breath.

"Will you still wear this on my birthday?" he asks.

I chuckle a little. "We'll see. I may go back and get you what I wanted. This was Alexa's idea."

Chapter 13

First Time

Looking around I think we have everything covered for Abel's special day.

"This turned out great," Troy says and pats me on the back.

I look around at the covered outside patio of Abel's favorite restaurant, The Brewery. "Thanks, Troy. I appreciate you getting all of the guys here and coverage for the station."

"Nah, don't thank me. It was nothing."

Troy gets pulled away by the guys, who are playing a game of pool. Vincent should be here with Abel any minute. They played a round of golf today and then planned on dinner, because I told Abel I got called in to cover a swing shift. We had a nice breakfast this morning and he was extremely understanding when I said I had to work. I just wanted to be able to get everything handled for his birthday. He has absolutely no clue about this

135

surprise party and what I have in store for him.

Turning around, I see Alexa as she is walking towards me with a huge smile on her face and says, "Hey, girl. This place looks great."

I embrace her in a hug. "Thanks, sweetie. It took all day to get everything set up. Thank God for all of the guys' help. It doesn't hurt how tall they all are either."

She laughs setting her gift down on the table. "I just talked to Vince; he said they're on their way here."

My stomach flips in anticipation. I'm so frickin' excited to surprise Abel and see the look on his face. Deciding to let the others know that they'll be here soon, I stand on a chair and whistle. Everyone stops what they are doing and looks at me. "I can't thank you all enough for being here today. I know Abel will feel the same. I just got word that he's on his way. Can everyone gather together so we can yell *surprise*? I'm guessing they'll be here in just a ..."

Alexa taps my leg and I look down at her. "They're here," she says.

"Never mind, he's here." I scramble down from the chair and gather around with the others. We are all intently watching the entrance to the patio and waiting for any signs of movement. Once the door opens, I see him and Vincent laughing and in deep conversation. As soon as Abel steps in, we all yell "Surprise!" and he looks at me in shock. Immediately a huge smile spreads across his face and he covers it with his hands.

"Holy shit, you guys!" he says dumbfounded, walking over to me. He doesn't hesitate wrapping me in his arms and devouring my neck. "Did you do all of this, kitten?" he speaks into my skin.

Locking my fingers behind his back I nod my head, breathing in his heavenly scent.

Pulling away he shakes his head and says, "You said you had to work."

"Guilty as charged; I lied. This took all day to get ready, plus you and Vincent needed some time together."

Troy and some of the guys come up and pull Abel away. I let him go and get things moving with the party; food, music, and drinks. The night is a whirlwind of fun. Alexa and I dance our asses off, and the guys join in too, and boy, can they move. Don't even get me started on the dance off that took place between some of the guys from the fire station. It had to be one of the funniest things I've ever seen.

As we all say our goodbyes out front of The Brewery, I'm excited to take Abel home. He is definitely tipsy. I would say this is the most I've seen him drink since we've been together. Tonight he was the king of taking shots. Grabbing his hand, we walk to my car and are the last to leave.

"Damn, Cara, your ass looks so fucking hot in those jeans."

"Why, thank you. You don't look bad yourself."

I reach for the door handle and he grabs my ass

squeezing hard and pressing my body into the car. I can feel his full erection pressing into me.

"The faster we get home, the faster I can make you come," I say.

He laughs and moves off of my back. I open the door and help him into his seat and with his seat belt. Walking around the front of my car, I look in and he is running his hands over his face. Sliding into my seat I ask, "Are you okay?"

"Yeah, babe. I'm good."

I pull out of the parking lot and make the quick trip to Abel's loft. He is quiet on the drive, so I reach over taking his hand in mine. As I cut the engine, he looks over at me.

"Cara, I feel bad I drank so much."

"Is that why you've been so quiet? You're fine, babe, it's your birthday."

I squeeze his hand and we make our way into his building. As we enter the loft, I lead him into his bedroom. On his bed is a red box. "You didn't need to get me anything else, kitten. The party was more than enough."

"But I wanted to. Now open it, please," I plead.

It doesn't take a lot to convince him and I can't keep myself from attentively watching him take the lid off and remove the red tissue paper. Tucked neatly inside is the clear cock ring, a bottle of lube, and the red nurse's outfit that I originally wanted to buy for him.

"What's this for?" he asks holding up the cock ring.

"It's a cock ring. I think it will be better if I show you rather than tell you."

He tilts his head to the side, "Okay. Why did you buy lube? We never use it."

I turn facing him and kneel before him on the bed. This is the most important part of his birthday present. I've thought long and hard about it and I'm ready. I want to give this to him and only him.

"The lube is the best part of your present. I know how much you want to take my ass. And I want to give that to you. I've never been with anyone in that way and I want tonight to be my first and with you."

"Fuck, Cara. I knew I shouldn't have drank so much tonight. You have no idea how bad I want that too. I want to fuck your tight, little ass and claim it as mine. But not like this — I'm too drunk. When we do it, I want clarity, so I can remember every single moment I'm inside of you. I want to remember every noise you make and how your body responds to mine. I want it all to be engrained in my memory, to hold onto forever."

His words are by far the sweetest he has ever said to me. I know the men I've been with prior to him would've jumped at this chance and not given two shits if they were drunk or not. "To be honest, I'm a little scared. I've never done anything like this, so I'm okay waiting as well."

"I've never been with anyone like that either, or ever

had the desire to. I told you before and I'll say it again, the things that you do to me are like nothing I've ever experienced. Look at how far we've both come together."

"I know and I couldn't be any happier."

He takes his hand and threads it into the back of my hair. "Can I still fuck your pussy tonight?"

"Of course," I say kissing him and removing the nurse's outfit from the box. I trot off to the bathroom looking back at my mouthwatering man.

I have yet to try this outfit on, but I don't think there is any way it could be any worse than the red fishnet one, and he loved that. The little frilly skirt barely covers my ass and my boobs are spewing out the top, but I guess that's the point. Walking out of the bathroom, Abel is leaned back on the bed with his arms stretched behind him and fully dressed.

"Did someone call a nurse?" I say with the straightest face I can muster. He nods his head and waves me to him with one finger. I strut to him like a runway model thrusting one foot out in front of the other, he licks his lips making me want his tongue on my body. In fact, I can't wait for it.

Once I reach him, he sits up grabbing my thighs, "I really like your skirt, nurse. Is it a required part of your uniform?"

"Yes, sir, it is. So, tell me what's wrong with you."

With a grin on his face he says, "Well, for starters I'm hot. I think I'm running a fever."

"Then let me help you get undressed." I reach for the hem of his shirt and have to stop to pry his hands off of my thighs. Once his shirt is off I begin the process of undoing his jeans and removing them along with his boxers. He stands before me naked, and I'm taken back by his perfection. Some might not like the tattoos or the piercings, but to me, they're what make him not only who he is, but beautiful.

"Do you feel better?" I say whispering into his ear.

"Yeah, a little."

He snakes his arms around my back. I walk us to the bed and push him onto it. He falls back with a huge grin on his face, "That's not fair, you were supposed to fall with me."

I shake my head and start to unbutton my small red top. Abel watches me with curiosity, like he's never seen what's underneath. My breasts pop free and are exposed to him, a growl from deep within him comes out and I know in that moment I have driven him crazy.

Bending over, I start to unbuckle my shoes, making sure that my ass is well in view of his face.

"God damn, Cara, I need to fuck you. I can see your pussy glistening for me because she's so wet."

Just when I get my other shoe off, he has me by my hips and is pulling me backwards to him. Removing one of his hands, he grabs his dick and guides himself into me. *Fuck, he's so big.* Sitting on top of him with my back to his front, I whimper and start to move, no longer needing time to acclimate. Our bodies mold and work together like they've become accustomed to. It's as if we were made for each other.

In the next moment Abel takes us from sitting on the edge of the bed to standing up.

"Fuck, this skirt is so damn sexy," he says into my neck.

Standing before him, allowing him to control me and us, I have the urge to touch him. Reaching behind me I grip his ass and hang on. Everything inside of me is on a roller coaster. My body is burning; I'm barely holding onto the orgasm that is growing inside of me. It's an angry demon that needs to escape.

Abel continues to pound me, with one hand wrapped around my hip and the other pinching one of my nipples. Before I can fight it any longer, Abel grunts, letting go, and pours himself inside of me. The pressure he is putting on my body in all the right places sends me over the edge. I let go along with him, coming while I hold his body to mine.

Chapter 14

Road Trip

Wandering through the mall, I think I have the last of everything I need for my trip home. I head towards the exit and my cell phone rings, I fish it out of my purse. Looking at the screen my stomach drops.

"Hey, Mom," I say.

"Cara, why didn't you tell me that you were bringing a boy home with you?"

"Because I haven't talked to you. And he isn't a boy, Mom. He's a grown man and my boyfriend."

Silence takes over the line. "Hello?" I ask.

"I'm here. What do you expect me to say to that?"

"I don't know, how about you're happy for me?"

"Oh, Cara, I want to be, trust me. But I don't want you to ever experience heartache like I have since I lost your father."

"So you're saying that you would rather I stay single forever to avoid the risk of heartache?"

"Yes."

"Dad dying was a freak accident. Plus, without Dad you wouldn't have Amber or me. I'm not going to stay single forever because he passed away. That's not what he would have wanted."

She takes a deep breath into the phone. "Well, he's going to need to sleep on the couch."

"Okay, Mom. Whatever you say. But please be nice to him. I really like him and I don't need you scaring him off. Think about Daddy and what he would want."

"Goodbye, Cara."

The line goes silent before I can get out another word. Ever since my father passed away she has gone off the deep end, needing control beyond anything reasonable. Thinking back on things, she has always been controlling, but more so now than ever.

My phone rings again, and looking at the screen it's her and I'm *not* going to answer it. I decline the call and get into my car. I start the engine and my voicemail beeps, so I check it as I start to drive.

"Cara, it's your mom. That boy needs to sleep on the couch!"

Oh my God, is she serious? She already told me that. Maybe Abel going home with me isn't a good idea after all. She's such a freak about meeting new people and has always been wary of strangers. I don't mean to bitch about her, because I really do feel bad. I couldn't imagine what she's gone through. Losing my father has clearly damaged her. But I will not live my life in the dark, hiding from happiness. I know loving someone is a risk; hell, I think I know that better than anyone. I've fallen in deep, time and time again, only to have my trust broken and my heart shattered. And not to mention I tried to stop things between Abel and I by fruitlessly fighting my feelings for months. Ultimately, I couldn't stop the path that was already laid out for us. In life, if you never take risks, then I truly believe you will never be rewarded.

I know my dad would not only be happy for me, but he would be extremely proud of me. He always told me to listen to my heart. As a child he taught me to be a free spirit. It allowed me to have a confidence within myself that other girls my age growing up — and even now — have never had. I vividly remember sneaking off with him to take long hikes, sometimes at night. This was something that only he and I did together. My mom was always so protective and scared of us hiking and going out late, so we said that we were going to the library. But we both wanted to be free and indulge in something we loved to do together. When we hiked, we would talk for hours and push ourselves not only mentally, but physically. The reward was the bond we shared, completing the journey together, and experiencing the spectacular view that we were lucky enough to see at the end.

Pulling up to my condo, I'm happy to see Abel waiting out front for me. *I really need to get him a key.* He's on the porch, sporting a huge smile. Walking up to him, I smile and the moment I'm close enough I kiss him, getting lost in the soft feel of his lips. He slows the kiss and I hug him tightly, nuzzling my face into his neck.

"Hey, are you okay?"

Without speaking, I move my head up and down. I don't want to get into what my mom said or how batshit crazy she is.

Pulling away, he holds my face in his hand and says, "Talk to me, baby."

"Do I have to?" I whisper.

"Yes."

Leaning into his touch, I say, "My mom called, and she is ... well, she's my typical controlling mom. And it got me thinking about my dad. I don't know; there's just a lot going on in my mind. I'm really nervous for you to go home with me and meet her."

"What did she say?"

"She asked why I hadn't told her that I was bringing home a 'boy.'"

"What did you say?"

"I told her that I haven't talked to her lately and you're not a boy, you're a grown man who is my boyfriend. She was silent and couldn't even be happy for me. She relates everything back to her losing my dad. She thinks that if I fall in love, I'm going to one day end up alone and hurt like her."

"How can she even relate the two? What happened

to your dad was tragic, but it was also an accident that can happen to any of us at any time. We could get into a car accident driving there. She needs to recognize that sometimes risks are worth taking"

"Ha," I can't help the laugh that comes out. "You're telling me."

"What if I could take your mind off of everything with your mom for a bit?"

"I would love that. What do you have in mind?" I ask cocking one eyebrow at him.

"Let's hit the road and I'll show you."

"You're going to have to help me pack then."

"Your wish is my command. I'll do anything you need this weekend."

Squeezing his ass, I pull him against me. "Anything?"

"Anything," he repeats nibbling my lower lip and then leaving kiss after kiss as he stares into my eyes. Before I demand that he fuck me, right here and right now on my porch, I fumble with the door handle in an attempt to get us inside. Once we are in. I look over at him and he looks sexy as fuck, with his hands in his pockets, wearing a thin, light blue t-shirt and a backwards hat.

"Do you want me to fuck you, Cara?" he asks with a serious expression across his face.

I nod my head as he walks up to me and says, "Good, because I want you to think of my cock inside of your tight cunt all day. I want you to imagine how good it's going to feel once I control you and please you any way I see fit."

I stick my bottom lip out. "No, baby, none of that. Now finish packing so we can miss traffic, and I promise I'll make your wait worthwhile."

I slap his arm and walk off pouting. Abel chuckles and follows me upstairs, slapping my ass on the way. When I come out of my bathroom carrying my tote worth of toiletries, Mr. Sex-on-a-stick is sprawled across my bed.

"Would you mind grabbing the bags out of my car?" I ask.

"Of course, do you need anything else?"

"No, thanks."

I finish up my packing, and when Abel comes back into my room, he empties the bags onto my bed, which I load into my suitcase.

"Geez, babe, do you really think you need to take this much stuff?"

"Yeah, I do. I have to have an outfit for every occasion."

"Shit, then I should've packed more clothes," he says jokingly.

"You're fine. I think this is everything if you want to load up and we can get out of here."

He takes my suitcase, kisses me on the nose, and goes downstairs. Looking around my room, I think I have everything I need. I grab my purse and trot downstairs myself. Looking around, all of the main lights are off. I leave the lights below the kitchen cabinets on and head outside, locking the front door.

Abel is organizing everything in the bed of his truck when I get outside.

"Ready?" he asks.

"Yup."

I hop in and he comes over closing my door. I wonder where we are going and what he has in store for me. I absolutely love surprises.

We pull away from my condo and I ask, "How long until we get there?"

"To your mom's is twelve hours, but you know that. To where I plan on fucking you all night long, about six hours."

My mind rushes to think what is six hours from here and on the way to Arizona. I come up with nothing romantic. But the thought of Abel and I fucking all night long has me so intrigued that I don't care where we go. He could park his truck on the side of the road and it would make me completely satisfied.

Once we hit the highway, Abel puts the pedal down. My eyes feel tired; work is finally catching up with me. Curling my legs underneath me, I look over at Abel. He's calm and confident and at such ease behind the wheel. His arm is draped over the center armrest and I lean to kiss it, breathing him in and enjoying his sweet scent.

Moving his hand he cups my face and precedes to move down my neck and back, finally resting his warm touch there. I moan and look over at his shorts as his cock is straining against the dark fabric. I sit up and move the center console, scooting closer to get an up close and personal look.

Touching my hand to his exquisite package, I meet my eyes with his only for a brief moment and then his are back on the road. I remove him from his shorts and a hiss escapes him. I don't waste a moment devouring him, tightly gripping his velvet skin with no restraint as I begin to move. Immediately my throat is warmed with a small drop of cum and I smile on the inside.

I move my hand and mouth in sync and feel his balls tighten. I know that he is close and I love that he is letting me do this. Pleasing him is one of my greatest indulgences. This is the least I can do to repay him for everything he has given me. There is such a long list and his coming on this trip is just icing on the cake. Abel growls and curses my name, bursting in the back of my throat. Swallowing, I continue my movements, slowing only a little … that is, until I hear the truck veer off over the rumble strips on the highway, which is loud as hell. I jump up and look ahead and see we are in our lane. I look at Abel and he has a huge smirk on his face.

"Damn it, you scared the shit out of me."

"Kitten, that was not my fault. You're the one who attacked me while I was driving down the highway at eighty miles an hour. I had to do something to get you to stop. It was either that or I was going to pull over and fuck you so hard you wouldn't have been able to sit straight for the weekend."

Sitting back in my seat I shake my head, laughing at his comment. Looking over at Abel, he is readjusting himself back into his shorts. *Serves him right.*

When he is finished and tucked away, he reaches for me. When he asks me to come, I always do. Scooting over, I get comfy, settling in my favorite place. We sit in silence and I concentrate on the sound of his breathing, thinking about how much my dad would've loved to meet him. I know they would've hit it off, since they have so much in common, and more importantly, they both want what's best for me.

"Baby, we're here," he says in between sweet kisses that awaken me. Looking around, the sun is setting and I don't recognize my surroundings. I'm snuggled in the same position I got comfy in, only this time the truck is stopped and Abel has both of his arms enclosed around me.

"What time is it?" I ask.

"It's a quarter after six."

"Where are we?"

"In New Mexico. Are you ready for your surprise?"

I nod my head and he kisses me, then slides out of the truck. I scoot over and put my flip-flops back on. Abel opens my door and helps me down to the ground. *Holy shit, it's hot here.* We turn to walk into our destination and standing before us is a huge Mexican-style stucco hotel.

"Oh, wow, this is gorgeous."

"Just wait 'til you see the inside and what I have planned for us. Let's get checked in."

Squeezing his hand I'm really excited. I've always wanted to stay in New Mexico. I remember mentioning it to him when we first met, but I never thought that he would've remembered or actually brought me here.

Check-in is quick and easy. Before we know it, we're headed on up to our room. Of course he booked a suite. As he opens the door and I'm floored by the modern layout of the expansive room. It has a true hacienda feel to it. The walls are teals and creams, and hanging from the ceiling in the living room are huge clusters of white bubble lights. Bar stools line the full white kitchen with a high bar. The floors are all wood leading into the bedroom. Which is just … oh my, this is amazing. The bed is white with a black illuminated headboard. Authentic pottery is strung in sets of threes hanging down over the nightstands with lights casting the most spectacular shadows.

I turn around and Abel is standing in the doorway. I

have wandered so far into the room and am just in awe of this suite. "Abel, this is fucking incredible. I can't believe you brought me here. Thank you so much."

He wraps his arms around me and says, "It's my pleasure, kitten. I take it you like your surprise?"

"Like it? I love it. I've always wanted to visit New Mexico."

"I know, you told me."

"I can't believe you remembered."

"Cara, I remember everything you tell me. When we are together, every new memory is carved into my mind. I know in the past I used women and never cared for any of them enough to want or have a relationship, but you make me want to do things like this. That all changed when you and your smart mouth showed up and flipped my world upside down. I want to prove how much you mean to me and show you that I'm never going to hurt you. I'm not going anywhere, so you better get used to things like this."

Those words are the purest I've ever heard. Looking into his eyes, in that moment I know I'm falling in love with him.

Chapter 15

Marla

I wake to the noise of the shower and Abel isn't beside me. I take a few moments to fully wake up and think about what the day holds for us, I wish we didn't have such a long drive. I feel like secluding myself in this room all day, but we can't. I step out of bed and look into the bathroom, Abel is fresh out of the shower and drying off. He's staring at me. "Hey, baby," I say and walk over to him, kissing him on the lips, looking up into his hazel eyes. I can't help but grin at him with the thoughts that run through my mind. "What?" he asks.

I lean down and kiss his stomach and then reach for his towel, tearing it off of his waist. That one movement causes his body to stir and everything below his waist awakens. His dick hardens, and I grab it, gripping it tightly and jerking back and forth. Leaning down, he kisses me, consuming my mouth and wrapping me in his hold. Slowing the kiss, he says, "Well, good morning to you, kitten," and rubs his thumb across my lower lip.

"Good morning," I say and I drop to my knees. Taking my pink plump lips, I engulf the head of his cock and move down. *God, I love pleasing him.* Still gripping his shaft, I work in unison with my mouth. I moan as I do so and those noises set him on fire. His body begins to shudder and I'm still amazed that I can take him so far, so fast.

Reaching down, he moves his hand and tweaks my nipple, working it between his fingers. I can't help but bow my chest out towards his hand. As we work together, I glide my hand up his body sending a shiver through him. Resting my hand below his chest, he places his on top of mine and comes violently, filling my mouth and thrusting his hips with the pace I'm keeping.

Once the trembles from within him stop, we make eye contact. Without speaking, I stand and he pins me against the wall; devouring my nipples, taking his time with each, showing them equal attention, as he flicks his tongue back and forth. Running my hands through his hair he lifts me effortlessly. I wrap my legs around his hips and he guides himself inside of me. My pussy is warm and tight like it always is. Keeping my back against the wall, he asks, "Are you ready?"

"Oh God, yes. Please fuck me."

He chuckles and gets a good grip on my thighs as I lock my fingers behind his neck and we both start to move. I watch our movements and how our bodies work together. I'm not quiet and neither is he. "Let me hear you, baby," he commands.

We indulge and moan while we fuck. Looking up, our eyes connect. I stare at him with my long blonde hair in my face like he likes. I begin to chew on my bottom lip and grip his shoulders; I know he's close to coming and I can't help but take him there. He presses me harder against the wall and I clutch his neck moving my hips with his as we fuck. I know we both like it rough and I love giving him what he wants. As he gives into the intensity of his orgasm, I scream, "Fuck! Abel!" and let go.

Watching him spiral out of this world pleases me as he comes for a second time. My body is covered in sweat and I'm now deadweight in his hold. He's exhausted me. But I could go all day doing this with him, even if I am drained. Thinking about our future and knowing we have a full life ahead of us, I am content. I no longer question Abel or what we have. Setting me on my own two feet, he tucks my hair behind my ear and I kiss him on the neck. I walk past him to turn the shower on and as I step in, I feel giddy when he follows me in. Closing the door behind him, I look up and he is giving me that look. I know he's not finished with me — but I'm not finished with him either.

My phone rings and I dig it out of my purse. "Hi, Mom."

"Cara, where are you? I can't keep dinner warm all night."

"We're close, Mom, only about fifteen minutes away."

"Oh, so that boy did come with you?"

"He's not a boy. He's a man and has a name, which is Abel. I would love it if you could call him by that?"

She huffs and says, "Oh, God. Like Abel from the Bible? The one who killed his brother?"

I can't contain the giggle that escapes. "Abel was actually the one who got murdered, Mom. But there are no coincidences with my Abel, I promise." I look over at him shaking his head.

"Just come in and take your shoes off when you get here. Dinner is ready and if you're a minute past 6:25, then we're eating without you."

"Goodbye, Mom." I hang up my phone and put my face in my hands. Just two days of her neurotic ways — I can do this.

"What was that about me being murdered?" Abel asks.

"When I told my mom your name, she related it back to the Bible. Like I've said before she is a little out there. Whatever you do, don't tell her that Vincent's real name is Kane, okay?"

He chuckles. "Got it. Now come give me some attention before we get there. I'm sure your mother won't let me near you and my dick is angry that we can't sleep in the same bed."

I want to straddle his lap, demand he pull the truck over and shower him with kisses, but I know that will make us late and I don't need the wrath of Marla right now. Instead, I begin by kissing, sucking, and devouring every bit of him I can. Making my way down, I start by pulling up his shirt and taking my time with his six-pack.

"Thank you again for doing this and for last night. I loved the hotel; it was way over the top and I don't know how to repay you," I say as I come up for air.

"Of course. It was something I've wanted to do for a while now and you don't need to repay me. I'm glad you liked it. Hopefully we can go back and visit again," he says putting the truck in park and kissing me behind my ear.

"This is it," I say, looking over at the two-story stucco house. It looks the same — dark brown with lots of cacti, a long walkway leading up to the wooden door. Abel grabs my hand as we walk inside.

"Hey, we're here." I yell and take my flip-flops off. Abel does the same and my sister, Amber, comes running to greet us. She doesn't take a second to stop and notice Abel as she crashes into me and presses me into the door.

Wrapping my arms around her, she smells like home, reminding me of when we were kids.

"Oh my God, Cara, I have missed the shit out of you. Why are you so fucking skinny?"

My mom yells out, "Watch your mouth, Amber. And Cara, make sure you both put clean socks on before you step on my floors."

We both laugh and I say, "No shit, she's still at it with the socks?"

Amber points to the basket with *brand new,* fresh, white cotton socks in it. I grab us each a pair and put them on as I say to my sister, "I miss you too, honey. I don't know how you deal with her. However, on a better note, Amber, this is my boyfriend, Abel. Abel, this is my sister, Amber."

He extends his hand to shake hers, "It's a pleasure to finally meet you. Cara has told me great things about you."

She skips shaking his hand and hugs him, thankfully not with as much force as she did with me. "I'm so happy that you're here. Cara has told me all about you and I couldn't be happier for you two."

I look to Abel and swear his face is a little red ... is he blushing?

"Thanks, Amber."

She smiles at us both, rocking back on her heels. "Should we go and see Mom?"

"After you, ladies." Abel raises his arm to gesture

that we lead him back to the kitchen. As we walk, my nerves are calmed by Abel's hand pressed to the small of my back. The last time I brought a guy home, my mom purposefully spilled food on him so he had to leave dinner early. Let's just say that was all the way back in high school. I don't know why my mom has always been weird about me dating, but she has. Then when my dad passed, she really lost it. Before we round the corner, Abel says to me, "Take a breath, kitten. It's going to be okay."

I nod my head and say, "Hey, Mom," looking at what once was a prim and proper woman. Standing before us is a woman I hardly recognize. She has aged and I can see that in her eyes. Her once-blonde hair is now mixed with strands of silver. It's now long and shaggy and no longer cut in her signature bob.

"Cara, you made it. And right on time, might I add."

Geez. *Thanks, Mom*, I kiss her on the cheek. "Mom, this is my boyfriend, Abel. Abel, this is my mother, Marla."

He extends his hand to hers, "It's a pleasure to meet you, Mrs. Savannah."

"Marla will do. You don't need to try and be proper with me."

"Marla it is."

"Alright, why don't you all wash up before you head out back? Please make sure you use the Softsoap and this hand towel to dry off with."

I roll my eyes at Abel as we abide to my mother's crazy hand washing rules before heading to the back patio. Stepping outside it's extremely hot, but this was my father's favorite place to eat, so it doesn't surprise me this is where she wants us to eat. As we all get settled, the sight of the backyard brings back so many memories. This is the house I grew up in. I remember him teaching me how to swim in this pool and how to ride my bike without training wheels on this very patio. Staring off, I get lost in the memories. I remember like it was yesterday …

Abel squeezes my thigh under the table, pulling me back into the moment. I look over to him with tears in my eyes and wipe them away. "Are you okay?" he asks.

"Yeah, I am," I say leaning over and planting a soft, tear-stained kiss on his cheek. I notice my mom looking at us and her expression is unreadable.

"Marla, the food looks amazing," Abel says.

"That's what Jack always said. Now don't be shy; you all can dig in."

I laugh a little. "Oh God, you don't have to tell him twice."

"I like a boy with an appetite," my mom murmurs. I look over at her with a glare in my eyes. "So, tell us Abel — what do you do for a living?" she asks.

"I'm a firefighter, ma'am."

I roll my eyes at Abel. "What?" he asks.

"You don't have to be modest here. Abel is the fire chief."

"No shit," Amber blurts out. "That's awesome! Do you guys really live at the fire station and slide down poles?"

"Amber!" my mom snaps.

Abel chuckles, "Yeah, we live at the station a few days a week, and there are poles that we slide down when we get a call."

"I need to come and visit your station," Amber swoons.

"Any time," Abel responds. "The fajitas are delicious, Marla."

"They were one of Jack's favorites."

I remember my dad always begging my mom to cook them for dinner. Even though he said he would eat them every night if she would allow it, she said we weren't going to eat them more than once a week. Looking at my mom, the pain is visible in her eyes as she drifts off to memories of him. She truly has *not* progressed in healing much at all. I mean, if she's still making his favorite dish when she despised it, then that shows something about her.

"How did you two meet?" Amber asks.

Like she doesn't know. I swallow my food and look at Abel. He catches onto my clue and starts talking. "I'm going to assume that Cara told you about Alexa and Vincent?" My mom nods her head as she tears a tortilla in half. "Vincent is my brother. Through the course of him and Alexa dating, I got to know Cara pretty well. Though I certainly had to work my butt off to convince her that we would be good together."

"There's nothing like determination to win a woman over," my mom says. "Your dad was by far the most determined man I've ever met." Tears gloss over her eyes as she excuses herself from the table.

"I didn't mean to upset her," Abel says.

"You didn't. She's actually being pretty normal," Amber says.

"I don't know what to think of her," I say.

Amber finishes chewing her food and then responds, "Regardless of how she acts, she has been excited for you to come home. Cara, she is always going to be controlling and a little cuckoo. That's something we'll always have to live with. When she tells you to wash your hands or take your shoes off, just do it. I've learned it makes things easier."

Nodding my head, I contemplate what my sister has said and put my napkin on my plate. I guess she's right.

"Are you sure that you're going to fit?" I ask, hot and ready. I've been waiting for this for too long. Finally tonight I can give this to Abel.

"Yes, baby, I'll fit. Your body is ready for me. Look at how it reacts to my touch; it will do anything I want." He has me lubed up and I'm scared — what if this goes horribly wrong? Closing my eyes, I focus on my breathing and hope for the best. But instead of claiming my ass, he nudges my mouth and I open my eyes ...

Abel is standing next to my bed kneeling with one leg on the mattress and his sweatpants pulled down a little. *I was dreaming.* "You're supposed to be on the couch."

Leaning down, he whispers, "I was, until I walked by your room after I used the bathroom and you were moaning like I was inside you."

Covering my face with my hands, I shake my head. Abel removes my hands and sprawls out on top of me. "What were you moaning about, Cara?"

"I was dreaming that we were about to have anal sex, and instead of going for my ass you went for my mouth, and that's what woke me up."

Speaking softly into my neck he says, "Too bad I woke you up then."

"Mmm-hmm."

"Well, I don't want to disobey your mom's rules, so I better get back to bed."

"No!" I say far too loudly.

"Why not?"

"I want you."

"Tell me more," he whispers, kissing my skin.

"I want you to make us both come, slowly and silently."

He moves to the side and takes the covers with him, exposing my body which is naked from the waist down. Not waiting a moment, he slides his hand over my sex and begins to rub in a parallel motion. He stops the sweet torture, removes his pants, grabs his cock, and presses himself against me.

"Will you lock the door first?" I ask, panting.

"I already did." And with that he sinks into me. Fuck, he's so good at this, awakening my body instantly. Once he is buried deep inside of me, he reaches under my shirt and grabs a handful of one of my breasts. I lift my shirt up so he can see and give the same attention to both of them. Rocking his hips in and out of me, he molds his mouth around one of the hardened buds and pinches the other.

Our movements are slow, and I love the fact that we're taking our time together. Both of us have become so good at this. Thinking back to the animals we were the first time we had sex, there was no way we could have had sex and kept quiet.

Taking my hands, I enjoy his body, slowly stroking every muscle, loving how it feels as he moves in and out of me. With each of his thrusts, he gets deeper and stronger. I tighten my pussy and grip his ass. Christ, I'm about to come, but I don't want to, not yet anyways. Looking up at him, I can't hang on any longer, and I let go silently but violently.

This pushes Abel over the edge. He buries his face deep in my neck and lets go, grunting into my skin with each thrust.

My hands can't stop loving his body and I don't want them to. He doesn't move and holds us in the same position, wrapping his hands under my pillow and staying put. I take this time and enjoy the connectedness that I feel. This is where I need and want to be. I couldn't be any more content than I am right now.

Chapter 16

Nana

"Are you sure your grandma is going to like me?" Abel asks me nervously.

I stop putting on my mascara and look out to him as he is dressing in my room. "Yes, she is going to love you. Don't be nervous, okay?"

He nods his head and pulls on a t-shirt. I look down at his jeans and I know that his outfit is not going to work. "You need to change," I yell as I flip on the blow dryer.

He comes into the bathroom and unplugs it, interrupting my routine. Flipping my hair up, I smirk at him and he is glaring at me. "Why do I need to change?"

"Clearly, you haven't checked the weather today, babe," I say walking over to him and then pulling his t-shirt above his head. "It's going to be a hundred and three degrees and the party will be outside for the most part. My Nana loves the sun; she can't get enough of it.

Plus, I was hoping we could sneak away for a hike later."

"How does Nana feel about tattoos?"

"Baby, stop! Why are you so worried? You weren't this worried when you met my mom."

"I just know how close the two of you are and her opinion of me is important."

I place my arms around his neck and look into his bright hazel eyes, smelling his sexy, clean scent. It's indescribable and makes me go absolutely mad. "I'm happy that her opinion means so much to you, I really am. But there's nothing she could say to sway the way I feel for you. I couldn't imagine not being with you — we have both come so far from the individuals we used to be, to now being an irrepressible twosome. I feel so lucky that we are on this journey together."

His hands remove my towel and roam up my body. Reaching my face he holds both sides and stares at me, "There's not a day that goes by where you don't inspire me. You've made me this way; you make me want to be a better person. I can't even remember who I was before I met you and quite frankly, I don't want to." Before I can respond he is kissing me and not being gentle. Reaching for his jeans I undo the button and search for the zipper. Once I have him in my hand, I get to work on the warm, silken skin of his shaft, stroking and tugging, imagining him deep inside of my wet core. He grabs my hips, lifting me onto the counter and setting me on the cool surface. Desire burns in his eyes as he looks at me. I'm naked and spread open for him, at his mercy to do what he pleases with.

He closes the bathroom door and clicks the lock. I watch him open me wide, wrapping his glorious mouth around my throbbing clit. Fuck, he's amazing with his tongue. My body shudders and it takes everything I have to stay quiet while he moves his tongue. My back is pressed against the mirror, and he has me pinned, legs open and held in his control.

I'm so close to coming, and suddenly he slows almost to a stop. Kissing and flicking my clit with his tongue, he dips two fingers inside of me. His shoulders flex with the movements and we both watch as he penetrates me, slowly moving. My breathing is heavy, and my body is squirming beneath his hold.

Placing his lips to my throat, he speaks into my skin, "Does it feel good when I touch you here?" as he rubs my clit.

"Uh huh."

"What about here?" he asks, moving his fingers to an unfamiliar spot low and deep inside of me.

Whatever he is doing sends me over, and I let go in the most intense orgasm I've ever felt. Gripping onto the counter, I hang on and let him take me to this place of pleasure. His hand is barely moving out of me and he is *not* touching my clit. He is only moving inside of me. I'm about to scream when I move my mouth to his shoulder to muffle my sounds. Once body starts to settle and stops convulsing, I lean back into the mirror. Abel's eyes are shining and a sexy grin is plastered on his face.

"What was that?" I ask breathlessly.

"That was your G-spot, baby."

"Holy hell, Abel that was …"

"Intense?"

"Yeah."

"Just wait 'til I am in your ass and get you off with your G-spot all at the same time."

I smile and close my eyes. This man is a sex god. I'm completely exhausted from that orgasm, that is until he fills my pussy with his hot, rock hard dick. I look down and watch as he slowly moves in and out of me. "Fuck, Cara, your pussy is tight."

Bracing my weight on my hands, I wrap my legs around his waist.

"Cara?" My sister knocks on the door and jiggles the door handle.

Abel and I freeze, looking at the door. "Yup, what's up?" I yell.

"Are you done with my blow dryer yet?"

"Almost." I say and reach for the plug, pushing it back in. It turns right back on and Abel starts to move.

I hear her say something through the door, but I can't comprehend it. I wrap my arms around Abel's neck and he holds me to him, walking us away from the door and over to one of the walls. The blow dryer is still buzzing in the sink and we get to moving again. He's standing with my body pressed against the wall, pounding me. I hope my sounds are muffled, but I really don't care. It feels so damn good. Abel is strong, and as I brace his forearms and lean back, every muscle within him tightens and flexes.

His mouth claims mine and takes control, aggressively parting my lips with his tongue and caressing every part of me. As we work together, I can't help how complete I feel at this moment. He is perfect for me in every way and shows me every day. He is my future, my light, and my sanity. I wonder what the future will hold for us. Then Abel comes inside of me, filling me with his warmth, while making his sexy noises. Tears fill my eyes with gratitude and I hold my body to his. I want everything there is to have with this man and I'll give him all of me in return.

He presses his soft lips behind my ear and sets me on my own two feet. "I think you just hit *my* G-spot, baby."

I smile and blink the tears away. "Good." I watch as he tucks himself back into his pants, turns the hair dryer off, and pulls his shirt on.

"Do you want me to return this to Amber?"

"Please," I say and wrap my towel back around me.

Looking at the clock on my cell phone, I realize we are running late and I now have to rush. I rummage through my suitcase and pull out a half black and half teal dress. I slide it on with a matching pair of teal heals and head back into the bathroom. My hair is a mess, so I twist it into a low bun and finish up my makeup. I hear Abel come back in and get changed. When I step out of the bathroom, his jaw drops.

"You're wearing that?"

"Yup," I say and spin around for him.

"Man, I feel totally underdressed," he says, looking down at his black Hurley shorts with his red tank top and flip-flops.

"Stop, you look hot as hell. And just so you know, I'm not wearing any underwear. So if we can sneak away and find a wall, you can fuck me like you just did."

"Damn, you're really satisfying my dick this weekend."

"Good," I say and kiss him, "because you always satisfy me."

We head downstairs to find my mom and Amber waiting for us in the sitting room.

"You can follow us there," my mom says in a sharp tone. She turns to walk off and Abel speaks, surprisingly, she stops.

"I can drive us all," Abel says. "My truck has a lot of room, and that way you ladies can all drink and I'll be the responsible driver.

"Cara, he's a keeper," Amber says shooting up from the couch and heading towards the door.

I know Abel is trying to earn brownie points with my mom and I give him credit for it. She nods her head and we all head outside, Abel helping each of us climb into his monster of a truck. "Sorry the truck's so tall," he says.

"Don't be sorry," Amber says. "This thing is bad ass."

Pulling away from the house, I program where we're headed into the GPS. The ride is eerily quiet minus the voice of the navigation as she says, *'Left turn ahead.'*

Thankfully, it's a quick drive, and Amber has helped by making some small talk asking about our life at home in Colorado.

Arriving at my aunt's house for the party, I'm struck again by its beauty. The house is a long, sprawling ranch with a tile roof and walls of signature Arizona stucco, and surrounded by the typical rocks and cacti. My little cousin, Zane, runs out and greets us, slamming into my legs. It makes me a little wobbly because of the heels I'm wearing, and Abel steadies me as I look down at the six-year-old who is grinning at me with his missing front teeth. He is my Aunt Chanel's youngest son and she is the youngest of my dad's siblings. Zane removes himself from my legs and grabs my hand, dragging me inside the house.

"How are you, buddy?" I ask.

"Good. I miss you, Care-bear."

"I miss you too, buddy."

"Are you going to come and stay with us again?"

"I'm afraid not, little man. I have a job now and a lot

of people depending on me back home in Colorado."

"Ahhh, okay."

"Is that my Care-bear?" my Aunt Chanel asks from another room. Zane gets distracted and runs off with some of the other kids, and I grab Abel's hand giving him a reassuring squeeze. My mom and sister separate from us and go into the living room. I don't follow them because I have to see Chanel. She is so much like my dad and we've always been close. Abel kisses my shoulder just as we walk in and she sees him do so.

His actions don't faze her one bit as she moves to hug both of us. That's just how she is, plus I have gushed over the phone about Abel, so she knows how happy he makes me. Pulling away from us she looks between Abel and I. "Abel, I hope you don't mind the hug, I'm just overjoyed for my Care-bear."

"Geez, will you stop calling me that? I'm not a kid anymore," I say.

Laughing, she says, "You're right, you're not. You are a gorgeous young woman. It's been far too long since I've seen you."

"Thanks," I respond. "I miss you too."

"Thank you for having us today," Abel says. "And I don't mind the hug."

"Oh, it's my pleasure. Now you two better head out back. Nana is dying to see you and to meet Abel. We'll catch up in a bit."

Heading outside there are crowds of people and we

are constantly stopped, greeted, hugged, and chatted up. There are so many people I haven't seen in years. It seems to take forever until we finally reach my Nana. She is sitting with her back to us on a wooden bench that Chanel put here in my dad's memory. It overlooks the red rocks, which is quite a stunning view.

She is knitting, and you'd be hard-pressed to find a time when she isn't. "Nana," I say as we step around the bench.

"Oh darling, you made it. You look lovely," she says embracing me in a tight hug.

Letting go of Abel's hand, I wrap both of my arms around her. She means the world to me. This woman has been there for me through every experience in my life whether it was good or bad. I can't think of a time when she couldn't make me smile; there is just something about her that makes everything better. Being in her arms makes everything right, regardless of the issues with my mom.

When we break our hug, I can't wait to introduce her to Abel. "Nana, this is my boyfriend, Abel."

She hugs him too. "So this is the one, Cara?" I feel embarrassed that he hears her question. I told her the other day that I felt like he was the one for me. "Yup, this is him." She grabs his hand guiding him to sit down next to her. As their conversation begins to flow, I sneak away. I know she is harmless and only wants to get to know him better. She's a little kooky in her old age, but in a good way. She's funny as hell, so I know they'll enjoy their time together. I look back over my shoulder as I wander off and she has her hand on his cheek. I can tell she instantly loves him, just like I do. Do I love him? Honestly I can say that I do. I can't believe I've fallen in love, and with no one other than Abel. Glowing inside with this realization, I flutter among the guests and enjoy myself while my Nana spends time with Abel. I steer clear of my mother as I notice she is drinking heavily. It feels like we just got here when the sun starts to set. Most everyone has left, and it has been so great to see all of my family members. The day passed with record speed and now we have to say goodbye. This is always the hardest part.

Hugging my Nana, tears fill my eyes. Every time I leave her, I feel like it may be for the last time, and the older she gets, the stronger that feeling is.

Scanning over my face she says, "Don't cry, honey. We'll see each other soon. I know there's a wedding in your future with the strapping, young fellow you've snagged. He may not want kids, but keep working on him. I told your mother the same."

"Nana," I snap. She smiles at my tone, I've never yelled at her and she knows I don't mean anything by it.

"Yes, dear, do you have something to add?"

Shaking my head, I'm unclear what to say to her. "Did he really say he wants to marry me?" I whisper.

She squeezes my hand and ushers me off of the

front porch towards the truck where everyone is waiting. "You'll have to wait and see. But you're right, he is the one for you."

Walking away I give one last wave to my family and climb into the truck. Amber and my mom are laughing when I get in, enjoying their own conversation. I stay quiet as Abel grabs my hand and I let my mind drift to thoughts of a future with him.

Does he really want to marry me? I mean, did he really say that? We've never talked about those sorts of things, so I'm kind of shocked to think that's where his head is. Do I want to get married, and even more — would I be any good at being a wife? I honestly feel dumbfounded, and then there's the comment my Nana made about how Abel doesn't want kids. I've always hoped for them one day. But honestly, I guess I could go either way. I'm not the warmest person and don't know how that would be perceived by a child.

If one were to ask, I would say that's part of the reason why I've always fallen fast and fallen hard, deep down I'm searching for the affection my mom never gave me. I wonder what Abel's reason for not wanting kids is. I'm sure it's legit, but I'm not about to go and ask him what it is just yet. He squeezes my hand and I look at him.

"You okay?" he asks.

"Yeah. Thank you for going today. I hope it wasn't too much for you to handle?"

"It was great. I really liked your Nana. She reminds me a lot of my mom."

"Really?"

"Uh huh. It was nice to visit with her and get that vibe."

I smile at him and shake my head knowing exactly what he means. "What are you two cackling about back there?" I ask, looking back at my mom and sister as they are laughing uncontrollably. My mom is clearly tipsy, as is my sister. They both continue to giggle, not paying attention to me or my question.

"Mom, did you hear me? What's so funny?" I ask.

She glares at me and waves me off. "I heard you, Cara. I chose to ignore you. Why doesn't Abel tell me why he doesn't want to have kids with you?"

"Oh my God, Mom. You can't ask people questions like that."

She has an evil glow in her eyes and I don't like it. "Abel, don't answer her." I forgot how crazy she could be, especially when she is drunk.

"Well, Abel?" she slurs. "Is Cara not good enough for you?"

"Okay. That's way out of line. I'm not sticking around for anymore of this. I hope you enjoy the rest of your weekend, because we're leaving," I say with authority in my tone to show her that I'm not only pissed, but I'm dead serious. I just don't get where her hateful attitude comes from sometimes. Once we get back to her house, we are packing and driving back. I'm not about to watch her down another bottle of wine before she calls it a night and becomes more belligerent.

Chapter 17

Little Red

After driving for six hours, we decide to stop in New Mexico again and stay at our hotel. Being back in the suite is a surreal feeling. I really love it here. It doesn't matter that it's midnight; I feel well-rested and not a bit sleepy. As I flip through the room service menu, I'm debating between chili cheese fries and a banana split. It feels good to be all alone with Abel and far away from my mom.

Abel walks out of the bathroom naked, drying his hair. He looks so yummy; there are small droplets of water on his perfectly sculpted, tattooed body. The towel is covering his cock, as I scan my eyes down him. His bare feet leave a trail of watermarks as he steps over to his suitcase pulling out a pair of sweats, grey, my favorites.

"Do you want me to order you anything from room service?" I ask.

Dropping the towel, he steps on it and then glides his sweats on. "Sure, kitten. What were you thinking?"

"Chili cheese fries and a banana split."

"Can I share that with you?"

I glare at him.

"Come on, Cara, you don't want to get that full, especially with what I have planned for you tonight."

"Fine!" I snap jokingly and dial to order our food.

He tosses a red box on the bed and sits next to it. Ooh, I love presents! Damn this woman for taking so long to take my order! Abel scoots behind me and starts massaging my shoulders. Mmm, that feels amazing. "Have them knock and leave the food in the hallway," he whispers.

I repeat his instructions and hang the receiver up. "What's this for?" I ask.

"Just for you. I wanted to give it to you the last time we came here, but I never got a chance since we crashed so early. I'm not letting another opportunity pass us by; open it."

He places the box on my lap and I notice it's the same box I gave him his birthday presents in. I open the lid and tucked inside is a satin bag. Reaching in, I pull out a bright red dildo.

I look at him surprised. "What's wrong with your penis?" I ask.

He laughs. "Nothing is wrong, at least I don't think there is. This one vibrates and lets both of us pleasure you. I want to watch you slowly slide it in and out of your tight pussy while I do everything else to you that will make you go wild."

I swallow hard and Abel watches me set it on the bed and then I stand to get undressed for him. I've never used a dildo, so I'm a little unsure of what to expect. Taking my time, I expose my breasts as I lift his soft, white t-shirt over my head. Before I can remove my pants he tucks his fingers into the waistband and pushes them down my legs. Slowly, I step out of them standing before him naked. Taking a deep breath, I reach over and pick up ... the little red dildo — that's what I'll call it — and slide it in my mouth, gradually sucking all the way up and then back down.

Abel's breathing skips a beat and I watch his hard dick pulsate through his pants. When I remove little red from my mouth it is soaking wet and I take it right to my clit, rubbing back and forth. I walk to the bed and lean back on the pillows.

"Take your pants off," I demand.

Abel complies and kneels above me as I rub the outside of my pussy. Both of us watch as I move it back and forth. Abel then touches the button on the bottom bringing the vibration to life. It takes my breath away, causing me to orgasm almost instantly. Fighting through the pleasure, I push the button again and this time it starts to pulsate. I can definitely handle this. As pleasure burns through my system, Abel takes little red from me and gingerly slides it inside of me. *Fuck, it's powerful.* "Take it back, baby," he commands, handing me the dildo and begins to pay attention to my breasts, sucking on my nipples, all the while deliberately teasing my clit.

Room service knocks on the door and neither of us falters from what we are doing. "Grab your cock," I tell him, and watch in complete lust as his skillfully trained hand wraps around the hard base of his shaft and moves back up.

"Jesus, you're fucking hot as hell," he says.

Closing my eyes, I enjoy the pleasure that is scorching through me. He plunges his mouth onto mine and I gladly accept his tongue. I moan in response and work myself close to oblivion.

He slowly pulls away and says, "Can I do that for you again?"

I let go and lean over grabbing his cock, jerking him just like he was. Abel pushes the button again on little red and I let go, calling out his name as he pulls the dildo all the way out of me and then pushes it back in, over and over and over. Slowing his movements, I stop twitching and he sets little red aside straddling me. His massive frame is pinning me beneath him, his hot dick is resting between my boobs and I grab each one squeezing them around him. Moving backwards and forwards he works himself between my breasts like he's inside of me.

I love watching him and how his body reacts to pleasure. Abel's noises begin and I know he is close to coming. His brows are creased as he watches his cock move. He's tucked tightly under my hold and it's hot to watch him. I don't know if he will actually come from this, but I want to please him, so I squeeze my breasts harder and am thankful for their size. A long moan escapes him, and he comes, spreading warm cum on my neck and chest.

Looking down at me with that panty-dropping smile, I remember how he dropped my panties a long time ago. He hands me a towel and I wipe off. Before I can say anything, I'm on my stomach pinned beneath him.

"Just so you know, kitten, I'm not done with you. After we eat, I plan to fuck you from every angle all night long. I'm going to make you come a dozen times while you scream my name and everyone in this hotel will know that *I'm* the one buried deep inside of you."

I'm panting from excitement and want to say fuck the food, but I don't. Instead I look at him and say, "Hurry up and get the food."

He stands and bites my ass cheek. Pleasure is the only thing I feel from his teeth and I know I want more. I imagine his teeth tugging at my nipples, and my pussy clenches at the thought. Maybe I do like a bit of pain with my pleasure.

I wake to warm kisses on my shoulder. Blinking a few times, I look over at Abel who is lying close beside me. We are both on our stomachs and I realize just how alike we are. His lips are so warm and soft, making me feel even sleepier. It's hard at this point to keep my eyes open.

"Come on, kitten, you can't sleep all day. Don't you want to get out and see the town?"

"But bed seems like such a better idea." I protest.

Moving his hand he snakes it between my legs. "If we stay in bed, then neither of us will rest, and after last night, my dick needs a break."

I can't help but laugh. "You think your dick needs a break? How do you think I feel?"

"See? My point exactly. Why don't we shower and you let me wash you?"

Nodding my head, I kiss Mr. Persistent. I watch him gets out of bed and walk away from me naked to shower. When I go to move, every muscle in my body is sore, so I take my time and stretch before I make my way to the shower.

Abel keeps his promise, washing me while I do my hair. I enjoy returning the favor, running my hands all over his vast body. Stepping out, we dry each other off and he asks me, "Do you want to eat breakfast here or somewhere else?"

"Let's get out of here and start exploring."

"Okay, I'm going to load the truck with our luggage and I'll meet you out front."

Abel dresses and leaves the room. I finish getting ready and head downstairs. He's waiting for me and we immediately start checking out the town – it's beautiful; I love the southwestern feel it has. The streets are lined with small shops, and as we round the corner, I see a cute, little breakfast café.

"Let's try there," I say pointing ahead.

Abel drapes his arm over my shoulders as we walk in sync to our breakfast destination where a young Hispanic boy greets us. Clearly, this is a mom and pop place, and I love that. We decide to sit inside since it's air-conditioned and there are not many other patrons in here.

"Rosa is your server. She'll be right with you," the boy says.

"This place is cute. I bet they have awesome green chili."

"Yeah, it's great, kitten. So I take it that's what you're having for breakfast?"

"Yup," I say, eyeballing the breakfast burrito and closing my menu.

"What do you want to do today?" he asks.

"Doesn't matter to me. Maybe we could head out and explore, shop a little, and wing it from there."

"Sounds great to me."

"Listen, I want you to know that I'm sorry for what my mom said to you. She was way out of line last night."

"Don't mention it, babe. She was drunk and that's to be expected. I can't blame your grandma for talking to her about our conversation, but I'm glad you intervened. I wouldn't want them judging me for such a personal choice."

Looking out the window, I think to myself about his words. What does he mean that he's glad that he didn't have to answer her? Rosa interrupts my thoughts, taking our order.

"When do you have to go back to work?" Abel asks.

"I'm on nights for the next three in a row. How about you?" I ask, adding cream and sugar to my coffee.

"I work the next three in a row too. At least we kind of work the same schedule when we get back. Do you want to stay at my place or yours this weekend?"

"It doesn't matter."

"Okay. Eat up, Care-bear, 'cause it's going to be a long day."

"Abel! Don't even start calling me that. I'm not joking with you."

He chuckles and digs into his food. We eat in silence and I focus on how grateful I am to be here. I really am lucky to have found someone like Abel and to have fallen in love with him. Holy shit, I can't believe I love him, and completely different from any of the guys from my past. How in the hell am I going to tell him? What if he doesn't feel the same way?

After we eat, we head outside and wander aimlessly from store to store. Abel keeps a firm grip on my hand, which I love. Both of us enjoy joking and being silly with one another. I take the time to grab Alexa and a few girls from work some souvenirs. Heading back to the hotel, I'm sad to leave. I don't want to go home and back to reality.

The truck is hot when we hop in. Thankfully Abel loaded all of our stuff earlier, so we could just hit the road. "You look tired," I say. "Do you want me to drive?"

"Nah. I'm good, baby."

Pulling away from the hotel, a sadness hits me, but I'm ultimately thankful we made this trip together. I need to figure out exactly how to express my feelings. I probably need to talk to my Nana, as I'm curious about the details of her talk with Abel.

Considering my track record and how I always scare guys off, I know I *can't* make that mistake with Abel. Both he and what we have mean so much to me. I know I'm already in too deep with him and it scares me, but he promised that he would *never* hurt me. Ultimately, all I can do is follow my heart. I just hope my trust is finally in the right man.

Chapter 18

Ready

Since being back from our weekend getaway, things with Abel have been better than I knew possible. That's not even the right word to describe how well the relationship is going. I guess I could say miraculous, marvelous, I don't know. Now I'm getting all corny and ahead of myself, but damn it feels good to be in an open and trusting relationship.

After work we are all going to meet at a local bar and have a few drinks for Jamie's birthday. Abel's bringing a few guys from the station and Jamie is demanding that we all dress-up as she's made it a costume party. Regardless of what I'm wearing, it will be good to have a few drinks and unwind.

"What are you wearing tonight?" Jamie asks as we finish up our paperwork before debriefing the night crew.

"Uhh, I thought you brought me something. I just have a pair of jeans and some heels that I'll change into with my cami and leather coat."

"You're so lucky I thought about you. It's nothing big, but I brought the accessories for either an angel or a cat."

Well, if she has a cat costume then I will definitely be wearing that. "I'll take the cat one."

"Cool. We can change here before we go. I can drive us if you want?"

"Yeah, that would be good." I figure I'll be going home with Abel, so I don't need my car; he and I can pick it up tomorrow. After we debrief the night crew, I think about how exciting it will be to be dressed up as *his* kitten.

Knowing Abel, he will get a hard on from just looking at me. Jamie and I head into the restroom and I slip out of my scrubs and into my black skinny jeans. I'm wearing black heels and a black cami to match. When Jamie comes flying out of the stall in her full on angel gear, I can't help but laugh. Especially because I'm struggling with the cat tail, so decide to clip it to my belt loop. The costume is black as well and I love the look; the ears look cute as I adjust them on top of my head of blonde hair. One last touch of eyeliner and lip gloss and I am on my way.

"Is Abel bringing any of his cute firefighter friends tonight?"

"Yeah, a few. I think he's bringing the single ones."

"Lord, please let one of them put out the fire

between my legs."

"Girl, you're crazy."

"There is nothing crazy about a good lay; especially when it's a one-night stand with a hot firefighter."

Getting in her car and pulling away, I think how little I miss those days; a fulfilling relationship is so much better. I couldn't image being on the prowl tonight. The bar is close to the hospital and doesn't seem too busy yet. We park and head inside. I check my phone and there's a text from Abel.

I can't wait to see you tonight. I plan to get you so drunk that you go home with me, lol.

As long as you don't mind taking home a stray cat, I'm game. Although Puss might be pissed.

WTF???

Jamie made me dress up as a cat.

Oh fuck yes. I can't wait to see this. I hope you plan on wearing those ears while you're naked.

Maybe I'll have you wear them while you're naked …

Not a chance. See you soon, babe.

"Do you want to snag a pool table?" Jamie asks.

"Yeah, that's cool," I say as we walk into the bar. We grab a table and I take my coat off, wishing I had more than my cami on tonight. I rack the balls and Jamie hands me a pool cue.

"I'm so glad that we came out tonight."

"It's your birthday, girl. I wouldn't miss it. It's going

to be fun for all of us to hang out together. I can't wait for you to really get to know Abel."

"I know, I'm excited too," she says, taking a shot at the balls. "How did last weekend go?"

I know what she is insinuating and I'm not really in the mood to answer. I planned on telling Abel that I was in love with him last weekend. I've tried a few times since our trip, and every time, I either chicken out or it doesn't feel right. I don't know why this is so hard for me, when it should be easy. I love him, plain and simple, so why can't I say the words? Maybe it's the fear of rejection or that he won't feel the same. There's always that chance he could respond with the dreaded "Thank you." Although in the back of my mind that seems unlikely and not like Abel at all, I'm still scared. Besides, every time in the past when I've opened up to a guy, he has left me. And I don't want that to happen with him. He has become everything to me.

"Earth to Cara?" Jamie yells.

"Sorry. What were you saying?"

"I asked you how last weekend went."

Before I can answer the question, Abel's familiar scent intoxicates me and his warm arms shroud me from behind. "Hey, kitten," he says, kissing behind my ear and moving one of his hands under the thin fabric of my top to rest on my hip.

Turning into his hold, I'm ecstatic that he's here. Damn, he looks delicious in his fire gear. "You dressed up," I say surprised.

"I heard there was a kitten that needed rescuing, so I had to wear the proper gear to be sure I was prepared for any and all situations, ma'am."

"Now aren't you just a charmer?"

"Only for you, baby."

"Thank you," I say and kiss him.

I pull away and take a moment to make sure everyone has been properly introduced. Jamie is smitten by one of the guys that Abel brought. He's new to the station and a rookie, but Abel says he's a hard worker. He's definitely into Jamie and I can't help but laugh when she takes his cowboy hat off and places it on top of her head.

"Do you want a beer, babe?" Abel asks.

"Sure. Do you want to play a game of pool for who gets to wear the ears later?"

"I told you, I'm not wearing those damn ears. Maybe I'll play you for a game of who wears the bow tie, but that's it."

"Fine, go grab me a beer while I rack the balls."

"Damn, I love it when you use the word rack and balls in the same sentence."

I slap his arm and he laughs walking towards the bar. I check my phone noticing a new message from Bridgette. Before I can text her back, I'm being pulled backwards by my tail.

Dropping my phone on the table, I reach behind me

and then turn around. It's not Abel. Standing before me is Jon, a sleazebag I met over the summer. He blew me off before we ever went on a date. He's clearly drunk, and I take a step back, but he doesn't give me space, stepping towards me.

"Get the fuck away from me, Jon."

"Damn, I've missed your mouth," he slurs. I can't believe I was ever interested in someone like him. "I'm so glad you're here. I lost your number and have been dying to talk to you," he says.

This time, more annoyed than ever, I push him backwards and he stumbles a few feet. "I told you to get the fuck away from me." I look towards the bar and Abel is nowhere in sight. I go to walk in that direction, away from Jon, and he grabs me by my hips.

Although he's drunk, he's strong as hell. Trying to fight free, I'm stuck. Then a fist comes flying across Jon's mouth and he's gone, replaced by Abel's bright red face. He moves hovering over Jon and starts hitting him again and again. All I can think about is Abel's safety and his reputation. Plus, at this point Jon is defenseless. Two guys pull Abel off of him and push him back towards me. He goes to lunge at them and I grab him around the waist. The moment I touch him he stops.

"Baby, he's out. Come on, let's go!"

There is a ring of panic to my voice. I'm terrified of what could happen if Abel were to get caught. Glancing at the two guys who pulled him off of Jon, I'm not sure who they are, but they both have a look in their eyes that says "Get the fuck out of here." My stomach knots up and I know we need to leave. Not only could he get in trouble with the law, but his career could be in jeopardy.

I turn him towards me and grab his face. "Baby, we need to GO!"

As the crowd around Jon builds, he starts to move and moan. I grab my coat and purse, along with Abel's hand and we go. On the way out, we run into Jamie. "Hey, where are you going?" she asks.

"Some asshole came onto me and things got physical with him and Abel, so we're leaving. I'm sorry, honey."

"Don't be sorry! Are you okay?"

"Yeah. I'm fine."

"You guys go. And don't worry, I know nothing."

The drive to his place is quiet. Neither of us talks, we just focus on the road ahead of us. Once we are safely in his building and riding the elevator up, I lean against the wall taking in a deep breath.

"I'm sorry, Cara."

"For what? Saving me from a drunken asshole? You shouldn't be."

"I should've reacted differently. I should never lose my temper like that. But since I've been with you, it drives me insane the way guys stare at you. I've been dealing with it for months and tonight I finally snapped. Seeing his hands on you pushed me over the edge."

Once we are in the safety of his loft, I couldn't be happier. However, I know I need to tell him that Jon isn't just some stranger. Even though, I don't want to bring this up to him, I have to. Trust is one of the most important parts of our relationship. I know better than anyone else how it feels to be lied to. I won't do that to Abel or put us in that situation, no matter how hard or awkward it makes things.

"Babe, stop beating yourself up. You absolutely should *not* have reacted differently. You should know that I met Jon over the summer. Nothing happened between us, but that's why he approached me tonight. He was drunk and said he lost my number. Obviously he didn't hear me when I told him to get the fuck away from me. But that's why I have you, isn't it? You have no idea how good it feels to be in this relationship where I know that you're here to stand up for me and with me no matter what."

I want to tell him that I love him, but I decide against it. I don't want to correlate those words with a conversation around Jon. Once I finally gather up enough nerve to speak them, I want the time to be right. In the pit of my stomach I know tonight is not the night.

Snaking his hands underneath my leather jacket, he pushes it off of my shoulders. With nothing but hunger scorching in his eyes, he lifts my shirt as well. I'm standing before him in just my jeans and my shoes. He goes straight for my breasts with his mouth, while unbuttoning my jeans.

Now that he can see my sex he clutches a handful of each ass cheek squeezing hard. He then removes his pants and tears his shirt over his head. Without speaking any words, I know what he wants and I'm ready to give it to him. I've waited long enough. Swiftly and effortlessly, he lifts me in his arms, still never taking his eyes off of mine.

Entering the bedroom he slowly lowers me to the bed. I lift my behind and remove my jeans. After they are off, I decide to bend over to show him what I want. Kneeling before him, expressing my wants, a low growl escapes him. He takes his soft hand and caresses my backside, slowly paying attention to the place no one has ever been. Taking his thumb, Abel licks it and gently accesses me. I moan in response to pleasure he's causing my body. I love the feeling and am eager for what this undertaking will hold.

He walks away from me and opens his nightstand drawer pulling out the bottle of lube I bought him for his birthday. Walking back over, he keeps his eyes on me and coats his cock with a thick layer, while I kneel in anticipation. Then he gently rubs his slicked fingers around my tight hole making sure I'm nice and slick too. Before he does anything else, he hovers over me and whispers into the skin of my neck, "Are you sure you want to do this, baby?"

"Yes."

His mouth touches my shoulder and I can feel the smile on his face. Turning towards him, he begins to kiss me. His cock is hot and throbbing against my ass.

I can't wait for this.

Moving down my body with his lips he takes his time giving uniform attention to all of the right places. Then he presses himself against me, wanting in. I panic that he won't fit, but he thrusts his hips gaining access. Stopping immediately, he asks, "Are you okay?" I nod my head and he takes his time with each inch as I adjust to the feeling. He fits, which was my main worry all along, and it doesn't hurt. It feels euphoric, as chills move over my body and pleasure spreads through every one of my limbs and my fingers and toes tingle.

A small whine of pleasure seeps out of me and it cues him to move. Abel begins, keeping things slow and steady. I can tell that he is on cloud nine and appreciating every bit of this.

"Jesus, baby," he moans.

Twisting his hand down to my pussy, he gives it extra attention. Then staying good on his promise, he slips two fingers inside of me, moving them to find my G-spot. The moment his fingers find my extra sensitive spot, I'm lost, a complete mess of passion. The combination of both places is too much for me to handle and I succumb to this place of ecstasy he has taken me, thrashing my head back and forth while screaming into the bed.

I wait for him to come as well, but he doesn't. Gradually he stops and asks me, "Will you lie all the way down?"

I comply, while his body weight follows, pressing me into the bed. My back is to his chest, and he grabs my hands. Interlinking our fingers and pulling them far above my head, his feet are locked with mine. I'm at his mercy, stretched out, lying here for him and his pleasure. His movements are slow and loving. Every thrust he makes is with purpose and meaning — the purpose his pleasure and the meaning our love. It doesn't matter to me that we haven't said the words. I love him and I can feel with every ounce of my soul that he loves me.

Chapter 19

Bilious

"Lex, it doesn't matter what you wear to the event you're going to be the hottest girl there." She peeks her head around the dressing room curtain and glares at me while I suck down my Starbucks. I really have missed these things. When I lived with Lex, I swear I had one every day. Since she moved out, I have it maybe once a month.

"It does matter," she says coming out in a dark red, floor-length gown.

"You know what I mean. Plus, you have that huge rock on your hand to show everyone that Vince is yours," I say, taking another drink. "Regardless, I think you should go with the red one or the dark blue. Oh, we should pick Vincent out a matching skinny tie to wear."

"Who are you and what have you done with my best friend?"

"What? It's a great idea."

"Fine, let's take these over to the ties and then we can decide."

While we meander throughout Saks looking for the perfect tie, I start to feel sick. Damn, maybe I shouldn't have drunk that Starbucks so fast. I take a few deep breaths and find a seat while Alexa checks out.

"Ready to grab lunch?" she asks.

"Sure." Although I feel like I could barf, I'm not about to ruin our day because I went all crazy on the Starbucks.

We decide on California Pizza Kitchen; it's not busy and they have a really good selection of pizza. Scanning over the menu, I decide to order what Abel likes knowing I won't be able to stomach much. I plan to drop the rest of the pizza off at the station.

"So how are things with Abel?"

I think before answering and can't help but smile. "Really good. As strange as it sounds, I love everything about him."

Alexa chokes on her soda and stares at me. "You did not just say you love him."

"I said I love everything about him. So, yeah, pretty much, I guess I did say that."

"Have you told him?"

"Hell no. I'm too much of a chicken. Trust me I've tried, but I haven't found the right time. Eventually it's got to happen, right?"

"Oh, it will."

"How's Vincent?" I ask.

"Amazing. He makes me feel like a princess every day."

I check my phone as it buzzes with a text from my sister. "Who's that?" Alexa asks.

"Amber."

"How is she?"

"She's crazy, young, and irresponsible. More so now that she hasn't found a job since getting laid off. I don't know what her deal is."

"That sounds like someone I used to know."

"Whatever, you snot. You were just as bad. Do you remember in college when we first met and missed the next week of school because we both drank so much initiating each other into our 'new friendship?'"

She laughs out loud, "Jesus, do I remember."

"God, those were the days. No responsibilities or worries."

"They were fun, but would you really change the way things are now to go back?"

Thinking about it, the only thing I would change is having my dad here. I wish more than anything that he never had the desire to fly. "Besides my dad, I wouldn't change a thing."

"I agree. Hey, have you heard from Bridgette?" she asks, taking a bite of her pizza.

"No. Have you?"

"Me neither. I've been meaning to call her. I'll tell

her to text you once I get a hold of her. I'm sure she's just busy wrapping up school."

I take a bite myself and the pizza absolutely nauseates me. I guess it wasn't the Starbucks; I must be getting sick. The waiter walks by and I ask him for a box.

"What's wrong with your food?" Alexa asks.

"I don't think it's the food. I must be getting sick."

"You better keep your germs away from me. I can't miss this event, or Vincent will kill me."

"He won't kill you. Maybe he'll tie you up and spank you, but I'm pretty sure that's the extent of his punishment."

"You know what I mean."

I text Abel while Alexa finishes her food. *I think I'm getting sick. I was going to drop off my leftovers to you, but I'm going to head home and rest.*

That sucks, baby. I'll try and leave early to take care of you.

I can't help but smile at his message. *Take your time, honey. I'll be in bed when you get there.*

I'll hurry. Let me know if you need anything.

"Who's that?" Alexa asks.

"Abel. I told him I wasn't feeling well and that I was going to head home and rest."

Alexa hands her credit card to the waiter as he walks by. "Alright, sickie, let's get you home."

"You don't need to pay for lunch."

"I didn't; Vince did. It's already done," she says taking back the card and receipt.

As we walk to our cars, she asks me, "Do you want me to follow you home?"

"No. I'm just going to crawl into bed."

She gives me a smile and a half hug keeping her distance. She's such a germaphobe.

"Good luck at your event," I say.

"Thanks, hope you feel better."

It's cloudy today and I walk fast to my car. It looks like we might get rain. I get in and turn the heat on because I'm feeling cold. "God, I hope that this passes fast."

While I drive home, a text chimes in from Abel. *How are you feeling?*

I wait to respond until I get there. ***Not too good. I just got home. I'm going to get in bed and try to fall asleep.***

Okay, baby, sleep well. See you soon.

I wake to my stomach rumbling; clearly it's mad at me for skipping my lunch. I should've known better. Rolling over I look at the clock and it's five thirty. Holy shit, I slept all day. I check my phone and there are no new messages.

Clutching the pillow tightly against my stomach, I know I need to eat. I pull back the covers and place my feet on the plush carpet. I get up noticing that I'm still dressed; I really was tired. Heading downstairs, I think of what to make. I decide to eat the pizza that I got for lunch. It sounds the best and will be easy to reheat.

I wonder when Abel will be here. I know he said he would try and get off early, so I hope that's soon. With my pizza in hand, I make my way over to the sofa and plop down. I skip flipping through the channels and decide to look through the DVR for something entertaining to watch.

Last's week's *Dexter* should do the trick. The nap must have helped, because I don't feel achy and I'm not as tired as I was earlier. The first bite of pizza is delicious; it sends my taste buds into overdrive. So I devour a few more slices and I'm officially full. Curling up on the couch, I get lost in the TV. That is until my stomach starts to turn and I make a run for the bathroom.

My stomach is pissed and immediately purges everything I just ate. It causes me to dry heave, although there's nothing left, but my body doesn't agree.

With my hands on the tile floor and my head resting on the seat, I just breathe. I hear Abel come in and close the front door. I can tell he is heading towards my room. Before I can speak to tell him that I'm in the bathroom downstairs, my stomach constricts, causing me to gag. There is nothing left for me to throw up, but it doesn't matter, my body still taunts itself.

Gag after gag and nothing is coming up. All I want

is for it to calm down. Abel presses his hand to my side and rubs tenderly. I lean into him and let out a big sigh. "I'm sorry you're still sick, baby."

"Thanks," I whisper.

After a few moments of my stomach seeming to settle, Abel asks, "Do you want to go and lie down?"

I nod my head and he helps me up, guiding me to my feet and then lifting me in his arms, resting my head against his chest. I enjoy the moment of calmness; my stomach's not angry and Abel's here. He'll get me through this. Once we are in my bedroom, he helps me to undress and get into bed.

Sitting next to me he rubs a hand over my face and then through my hair, all the while calming me with shushing noises. The last thing I feel before falling asleep are his lips against my temple and hear his words, "Sleep well, kitten."

Chapter 20

My Kitten

- ABEL -

Watching Cara get sick kills me. Her breathing is calm and she is fast asleep. I don't want to leave her, but I need to eat. Fuck, who am I kidding? I always need to eat. I carefully get up from her bed and walk towards the door. Looking back, I take one last glimpse before I pull the door shut as quietly as I can.

Walking downstairs, I see the plate and leftover pizza that must have made her sick. She only ate a few pieces so I'm sure she will be starving when she gets up. I look in the fridge and there's not much in there that will be easy on her stomach. I always remember my mom telling me when I was sick to stick with the BRAT diet: bananas, rice, applesauce, and toast.

In my chicken scratch handwriting I leave a note on the counter.

Ran to store to grab some dinner and medicine for you. Call me if you wake up.

Hopefully she doesn't wake. I leave, locking the front door with the key she gave me, and jog to my truck. I wish this damn vehicle weren't so loud; I hope it doesn't wake her. Pulling away, I speed to the store. I'm on a mission to take care of my kitten, as well as feed myself.

I really have become such a sap. As I park and hop out of my truck, I pull my hat down low and grab a cart. My phone rings and I notice it's my battalion chief. *Damn it.*

"This is Abel," I answer in a sharp tone.

"Hey, Abel, it's Tom. Do you have a quick moment?"

Tom is my boss and if he calls, you make time for him. I'm the youngest Chief in the district and have to make it a point to prove to him that my age doesn't matter. "Yeah, of course. What's up?"

I decide to save time and keep shopping while we talk. "I have some bad news. We lost a group of guys last night at one of our sister stations. It was a freak accident. They all went into a building, and for some reason, some asshole had a ton of propane tanks. Well, as you can imagine, they were unaware and once those suckers went off they were like bombs. Needless to say, no one came out of the building.

"We've been asked to send a group of guys over

there. I can't send a bunch of rookies without a leader. They are going to need a Chief and I know you're the man for the job. You can take two guys from your station with you and there will be others from the area joining. They need you there by Tuesday; that's when the current relief guys have to leave. Can you do it?"

This is my moment to prove I'm worthy of my post. As horrible as I feel leaving Cara, I'm sure she will feel better by then. "Yeah, Tom, I can do it. Let me call the station and I'll let you know who is coming with me."

"Thanks, Abel. I knew I could count on you."

"No problem," I say, hanging up.

I'll have to handle calling the station later. Right now I have to get back to Cara. Looking in the cart, I don't even know what I threw in there. So I make a mental note of the BRAT diet, as well as ginger ale and Tums. I think I have it all.

While I wait in line at the checkout, I text Troy. ***What's up dude? Did you or the guys at the station hear about what happened?***

The clerk is some douchebag kid who is far too slow for my liking. I'm thankful when the manager calls me over to another lane and I hope can get me out of here quickly. Troy texts me back. *Yeah, we saw it on the news. It was insane. I feel bad for those guys and wish we could help.*

I know it sucks. Funny you should mention help. Tom called and asked me to assemble a team to head over there and help out at their station. I

don't know all of the details, but would you be down to join?

Yeah, man, count me in.

Cool, do you want to ask the guys at the station and see who else wants to join?

You got it. I'll call you later.

The cashier checks me out in a breeze. The douche on the other lane is still lost. I just have to chuckle as I watch him struggle looking for the bar code on a box of cereal. What an imbecile. I'm thankful to be on my way out of here. I load up the groceries and drive off in the direction of my girl. I really hope that she's still asleep; Cara needs to rest in order to feel better. My mind envisions her vomiting and it makes me ill.

Pulling in her driveway, I kill the truck as soon as it's in park. The groceries are light and I grab them all in one trip entering the house as quietly as possible. She's not in the living room as I set the bags down. My note is in the same spot as I left it, so I'm sure she's still asleep.

I unload the groceries and once everything is away, I make myself a sandwich and grab a bag of chips heading to the couch, but before I can eat, I need to check on her. I slip off my shoes and walk upstairs to keep quiet. I push her door open softly, and she is just as I left her — quiet, comfy, and peaceful. She really is the most beautiful thing I've ever seen. My dick starts to stir thinking of her naked below the covers, so I close the door and wipe the shit-eating grin off of my face. I'm one lucky bastard. Flipping through the channels, I stop on ESPN to watch the latest news on the upcoming NFL season.

Damn, this sandwich tastes delicious. Tearing open the bag of chips, I notice I forgot a drink so I head back to the fridge and grab a beer. My kitten knows how to keep this thing stocked with alcohol and that's one of the things I love about her.

I really need to grow a pair of balls and figure out how to tell her how deep I'm in this. I'm just scared that she doesn't feel the same. I should call my dad and ask him for some advice. I know my brother has been through it, but he blurted out the words in the middle of a fight with Alexa. He doesn't regret them at all, but that's not the point. For me, I want to do it in a different way. My kitten deserves a special memory when I tell them to her.

I can't believe I'm even considering telling her. If you were to have asked me six months ago what my opinion was of love, I would have told you to piss off and that I don't have time for it. I hear the door open upstairs and standing on the landing looking as stunning as ever is Cara. She takes my breath away, wrapped in her comforter, hair a mess, and cheeks flushed.

She comes down the stairs and I sit back patting my chest with open arms. She crawls in my lap and rests her head on me. "Hey, baby. Are you feeling any better?"

She shrugs her shoulders. "I don't know, maybe a little."

Pushing the hair out of her face, she looks at me with an exhausted expression. "I ran to the store and grabbed a few things my mom used to give me when I was sick with the flu."

She nods her head and says, "You didn't need to do that. I can just have some toast."

"Yes, you can, so I bought you some whole wheat bread. What do you say, do you want to try a piece?"

"Please."

Her voice is raspy and I'm hoping that the toast and some ginger ale will do the trick. As I get up and leave her on the couch, I look back — she's lying with her eyes closed. I don't care what she says, I'm not buying that she's feeling better.

I pop the toast in the toaster and pour her a small glass of ginger ale. I only toast the bread lightly, because I'm going to give it to her dry, unsure if her stomach can handle butter. Walking back over, I hand her the drink and she looks at the light tan liquid questioningly. "It's just ginger ale, babe. Take a sip."

"Thank you," she says, listening to me and then exchanging her drink for the plate of toast.

"Take small bites, okay?"

She nods her head and I flip through the channels landing on a new episode of *The Deadliest Catch*. We've been up to date on all of the episodes this season so I know she'll enjoy watching it with me.

I watch her slowly nibble the toast; finally she sets

the empty plate on the table and trades it for another small sip of ginger ale. While we both sit in silence and enjoy some quiet time together, I'm thankful that she is feeling better. That is until she bolts up and runs to the bathroom, leaving only the comforter behind. Once she is out of sight I hear her throwing up.

Fuck.

I run in after her. She's kneeling on the floor in front of the toilet dry heaving. Her naked body looks so frail. I rub her back and grab her hair for her. She drops her arm as if her body doesn't have an ounce of energy left inside. As much as I wish it was me who was sick, it's not. I try and think back to what she has eaten over the last few days that would have made her this ill and I come up empty handed. I bet she got this from work, always dealing with so many sick and dirty people.

Finally the heaving stops and she hangs her head lethargically. I can't watch her sit here anymore. Scooping her up in my arms comforts me and I hope she feels the same. I carry her upstairs and lay her gently down in bed. I lie down next to her and do what I can to calm her, stroking my fingers delicately over her back, making small gentle circles until she falls asleep. I'm not far behind her. Her tiny breaths and warm body relax me.

I wake up and glance at the clock, it's eleven in the morning. The sun is bright and illuminating Cara's white room. I look down at my kitten; she is tucked in a tiny ball against me. Naked and pure. I'm pleased that we both slept through the night. Leaving a tiny kiss on the top of her hair I slither out of bed. I need to handle calling the station. I'm sure Tom's wondering why I haven't contacted him.

Before I leave the room, I grab a pair of sweats and a t-shirt out of the drawer I now keep things in and swipe my phone out of my jeans pocket from the floor. Quietly I leave and head downstairs. I start to brew a pot of coffee and text Troy. My phone rings and I answer it. "What's up, dude?"

"Hey, it's Troy. Sorry I didn't get a chance to call you last night."

"It's cool. Did you talk to the other guys about going to help the other station?"

"Yeah, Matt is going to come with us. We were wondering when you wanted us to be there?"

"We need to be there tomorrow. If that's alright with you guys, let's say eight o'clock?"

Warm, tiny hands wrap around my stomach from behind and I know that she just heard me. I wanted to sit down and tell her that I was leaving, because I could be working for at least a week straight. It's too late now. I turn and kiss her on the nose. A frown is spread across her face as she looks up at me and I know why.

214

"That's good with me."

"Cool, I'll see you guys tomorrow."

Hanging up the phone, I take a breath and try to read her expression. She looks better. She's wearing a tank top and some of my sweats. Her hair is messy and in a bun on top of her head, a few small pieces are framing her face and I can't stop myself from moving them out of the way.

"You look like you're feeling better," I say.

"I am, thank you. I guess all I needed to do was get that crap out of my stomach and a good night's sleep. Who was on the phone?"

"It was Troy. I got a call from Tom, my Battalion Chief, yesterday when you were sleeping. We lost a group of guys at a local station. He asked me to assemble a team to go help out."

"Oh," she says with a worried expression on her face. "How long will you be gone?"

"I don't know, probably a week. I need to call Tom. I know he will have some new details on the situation."

"Okay."

"Do you feel like eating anything or having some coffee?"

"No, thanks, I'm going to keep things light today. You make your call and I'm going to hop in the shower."

I nod my head and kiss her behind her ear. She walks off pushing the loose hair behind her ear again. I call Tom as the coffee stops brewing and I pour myself a cup. Hammering out the details with him is easy. The short and skinny of the situation is that he doesn't know how long we'll be gone for. He's hoping no longer than a week, like I thought, and I couldn't agree more. I take my coffee upstairs and hear the shower's still on. I quickly undress and walk in the bathroom. Cara's silhouette catches my eye as she rinses her hair. She is the most gorgeous woman I've ever seen. Her perky boobs are pushed out and her back is arched, accentuating her ass.

I pull the door open and she looks over at me, moving out of the way to allow me to step in. The water is perfect just like we both like. She hands me the bar of soap and I start to wash myself with it. As much as I want to do more, I don't want to push her. My mind easily drifts as I stare at her body. I want to wrap my mouth around each of her nipples and then slide my hand in between her legs.

She looks me in the eyes and moves her arms around my neck. As we stand staring at one another, our chests touch and move as we breathe. My dick is getting hard and growing between us. "Sorry about that," I say.

"That's not something you should be sorry for," she says kissing my neck and then starts to suck in the way only she can. I close my eyes and can't help my hand from grabbing her nipples. The hardened peaks make me ready for her. Sucking on my neck, she moves her hand and clenches my dick, tugging and rubbing him on her clit.

I can't stop myself anymore and say, "Guide him inside of you, so I can slowly fuck you."

She listens to my command, like she always does. The pleasure spreads throughout my body as I slip inside of her. Once I'm buried deep, I wrap my arms around her tightly, probably more so than I should have. But I can't control myself with her – she's my greatest indulgence. Slowly I pull out and the slickness of her pussy mixed with the water causes a ripple effect. As I move again, the same ripple happens, causing us both to moan. I continue my movements, in and out, over and over, taking my time with each thrust. Our noises become a pitch higher, and we both hang on to our releases by a thread. The orgasms that are pulsing through our bodies are too much to handle. My balls tighten and I know there is no going back. I keep my movements steady and let go.

Fuck, her pussy is tight.

I pump myself inside of her using slow, long strokes. Her body trembles under my hold as she cries with pleasure. Her eyes are closed and she has her bottom lip tucked tightly in between her teeth. A few moments pass while I stare at her. She's a frozen statue of perfection being held in my arms, tiny trembles moving through her from what we just did.

In that moment, I want to tell her that I love her. But I don't, I puss out, and instead pull my dick out of her and turn off the water. Stepping out, I hand her a towel and then grab one for me.

"So you are feeling better?" I ask.

"After that, how could I not be?"

"I'm being serious, babe."

She dries herself off and says, "Yeah, I feel good. Did you talk to Tom?"

"Yeah, he said we need to be at the station tomorrow and we should plan on at least a week."

She nods her head and walks into her closet. "Okay. Will I get to see you at all while you cover there?"

"I'm not sure, but you know I'll be thinking about nothing but you. And I'll text you like a first class stalker."

"You better only be thinking of me," she teases and throws her towel out to me.

"You know it, kitten. Do you mind if I run home and pack some stuff for the week and feed Puss? Then we can spend our last night together."

"Sure, that would be great. I need to do my laundry and run to the bank."

"Cool. Would you mind feeding Puss while I'm gone?"

"Of course I will," she says.

I get dressed and walk into the bathroom. Cara is fighting with her hair and I just have to laugh at her.

"What are you laughing at?" she scolds.

"You and your hair?"

"You better wipe that smirk off of your face or I'll beat you with my hairbrush."

I put my hands up to signal defeat. She points her brush at me and I kiss her cheek. "I'll be back soon, baby."

As I walk out of her condo, I lock the front door behind me. Deciding to call my dad while I drive home, I dial and he answers right away.

"Hey, Dad."

"Son, is everything okay?"

I chuckle, knowing I've earned the question. "Yeah, why wouldn't it be?"

"Just checking. I never hear from you anymore. How's my oldest son?"

"I'm good. Listen, I need your advice. I want to tell Cara that ... well, that I think I love her and I don't know how to say it."

"I can tell you *not* to start the conversation out with, 'I think I love you.'"

"You know what I mean. I've wanted to tell her for a while, but I don't know how or what the right words are."

"I get that those situations are hard, but I honestly think going into them with an open mind and no agenda is best. You're overthinking all of this. When it feels right, speak from your heart. Let every word come as it does. That's what I did with your mom."

"Really?"

"Yeah. I looked at her one day and couldn't stop the words. They just came out. That's what happened with your brother too. Don't think so much about it, Son. The time will come and you'll know when it's right."

"I never thought about it like that. Thank you."

"Of course. Speaking of, how is Cara?"

"She's okay. She had the flu, but is finally feeling better today. I think she got it from the hospital."

"She's not pregnant is she?"

"Oh, hell no. She's better today. Why would you even ask? It was just a twenty-four hour bug."

"Just thought I'd ask. Send my love to her and tell her that I'm happy she's feeling better."

"Will do, Dad. Thanks."

After we hang up, I think back to his comment. Could she be pregnant? God, please no, I'm not meant to be a dad. I've been down that road once and vowed to *never* do it again.

Chapter 21

Choices

My bags are packed and I have one errand left. After that I can't wait to spend one last night with Cara. The drive across town takes about thirty minutes, but Vincent promised me this was the best jeweler for what I need in the quickest turnaround time. As I pull in and park, there aren't any other cars. I walk into the small, standalone building in the center of the strip mall parking lot. I don't see anyone working and start to look through the cases.

"Sorry, I didn't hear you come in."

I look up to see a short, elderly man who has a thick pair of glasses on. "It's okay, I was just looking around."

"What brings you in?" he asks.

"I was hoping you have infinity bracelets"

"Oh yes, I do. They're on this side." He walks to the other counter and I follow him across the store. Vince was right — tucked in the case is a huge selection. I'd heard about these and never knew exactly what they were 'til I talked to Alexa. I scan over the selection of bracelets with the well-known figure eight design, searching for the one and then I spot it.

It's gold, like Cara loves, with a double infinity symbol, both of which are diamond encrusted. It leads into a thick gold band — exactly what I want. "Can I see that one?"

"This is by far one of my favorites," he says as he hands it to me. Holding it in the palm of my hand, the metal is heavier than I expected. Looking it over, it's perfect.

"I'll take it. I heard you also do engraving?"

"Absolutely."

"Can you do it for me now? I can pay extra for the rush."

He looks at the clock, and then hands me a pad of paper and a pen. "I would be happy to. Just jot down what you had in mind and I'll do it while you wait. Maybe fifteen minutes."

"Great, thank you so much."

While I write what I want the engraving to say, he says, "I take it this is for someone special, considering you haven't asked me the price."

I hand him the note and say, "Yeah, she is special. When it comes to her, money doesn't matter. She has changed my perspective on life, so little things like this are the least I can do."

"That doesn't happen often these days. I'll have it

right out for you."

"Thank you. Do you think all of the words will fit?" I ask.

He looks over the note. "Yes, sir, I believe they will. Let me key it in the computer to be sure."

While I wait and check my phone, I have a text from Alexa. **_Everything good there?_**

Yup, I found the perfect one. Cara's going to love it.

The words fit and the bracelet looks amazing. I can't wait to give her something *real* as a symbol of my love. Today I'll finally be able to speak the words I've been scared of saying for far too long. The drive across town is quick and I'm anxious as I pull into her driveway. Before I head inside, I take a deep breath and clutch the box containing her bracelet in the palm of my hand. I know I can do this and she is going to say the words in return. I just know it. But Cara is nowhere to be seen. "Baby?" I yell.

"I'm up here."

Excitedly I jog up the stairs. She's not in her room so I go into the bathroom. She is sitting on the corner of the tub. Her head's hung low and she doesn't make eye contact with me.

"Hey, are you feeling sick again?"

She shrugs her shoulders and I notice the box sitting next to her.

Please don't let that be what I think it is.

"You've got to talk to me, Cara. What's going on?"

She hands me the test that she's holding and looks at me with guilt-filled eyes. Her cheeks are flushed and tear-stained. I take it from her and clearly printed across the digital screen reads *pregnant*. The box I'm holding slips from my grip and wallops on the tile floor. Looking down at it, I'm frozen. My body goes numb and it feels like all of the blood is rushing out of me. Suddenly it looks miles away, as my vision narrows and my heart starts pounding in my ears. My eyes move back to the test in my hand and I can see out of the corner of my eye that she is staring at me.

Fuck, NO! This is not possible. Why is this happening to me again?

"Say something," she begs.

I just shake my head, trying to calm the adrenaline spiking through every nerve ending. Finally I blurt out, "How did this happen?"

"I don't know. We've never used protection."

"But you told me you were on the pill."

"I am on the pill, but it's not 100% effective."

"Damn it, Cara, you knew I didn't want kids." There is anger in my tone but I can't help it. One of my worst fears is coming true. Again.

Tears stream down her cheeks like waves of the ocean and she places her face in her hands. "I know," she whispers.

I can't control the anger inside of me as I chuck the test at the mirror. It bounces off the glass and pings across the room. Cara flinches but doesn't look up at me, and I turn and walk away. As much as I love Cara it scares me how good it feels to get away from her.

Fuck. Fuck. Fuck. I slam the front door and get in my truck not thinking twice as I start it and drive away. I'm not sure where I'm heading, but I need to be alone.

Why didn't I see this coming sooner or catch the warning signs? Maybe if I wasn't so blindsided I could handle things better. Even when my dad mentioned it I didn't think for a second that it could be true. I decide to go home and stop at the liquor store on the way. I grab one thing — a bottle of Patrón. I know that I'm going to need this to get through the night, then hopefully work can consume me for a while as I figure out what to do.

I pull into the garage like a maniac and storm inside, on a mission to get into my loft and drinking to calm my nerves. As I ride the elevator up, I crack open the bottle and take a swig. When I open my front door and walk in, I can smell her scent. Normally it comforts me, but now it scares me. I'm about to ruin her life and there's nothing I can do. As control of the situation continues to be stripped away from me, I take another swig hoping to dull the pain.

I avoid looking into my bedroom and the spot where we could have created a life and throw myself on the couch. Taking another long pull, I allow the sting of the alcohol to roll down my throat. Hopefully after a few more shots the pain will subside and I can focus on what to do.

My phone starts to buzz and I look down at it. It's Cara, her picture displayed on the screen. It is by far my favorite — she's topless lying face down in her white bed with her hair covering half of her face and her chin resting on her hand, which is resting on her arm. *I can't talk to her.* I decline the call and take another drink.

Sitting there I mind fuck myself and come to the same conclusion every time. I can't be a dad; it's not in the cards for me. After God only knows how long and half a bottle of Patrón, the shots catch up to me and I get tired. The alcohol mixed with the stress is a combination that sends me off. Blackness takes over, which is a relief compared to the turmoil that is racing through my mind.

"Is Abel Mileski available?"

"Yeah, this is him."

"Abel, this is Doctor Larson with St. Luke's Hospital. Do you know an Abigail Riley?"

"Yeah, she's my girlfriend."

"She was just admitted to the ER and your number is the last one called from her cell phone."

"What happened? Are she and the baby okay?"

"I need you to come down here ASAP."

"Please just tell me if she's okay?"

"Sir, please get down here."

I hop in my car and fly over to the hospital driving as fast as I can. Lord, please let her and the baby be okay. Pulling up to the emergency entrance, I leave my car in the loading zone and run inside.

"I'm here to see Abigail Riley."

The woman behind the desk scans her screen and shakes her head. "I'm sorry, sir, we don't have an Abigail Riley here."

"I was just called by Dr. Larson. He said she was here. Call him," I scream.

"Yes, sir."

I run my hands through my hair and pace back and forth, saying a prayer. The ER doors open and out comes a middle-aged doctor with longish red hair and freckles. "Abel?" he asks.

"Yes. How is she?"

Concern washes across his face. "Follow me," he says and we begin to walk. "Cara was brought in earlier with a lot of stomach pain."

"Cara?" I ask.

"Yes. Your girlfriend, Cara Savannah. You told me that over the phone."

I swallow hard and shake my head knowing already what is coming next.

"After you told me she was pregnant, I checked. She was indeed pregnant but it was a tubal pregnancy. We rushed her back for surgery, but it was too late. She had lost so much blood and had a heavy amount of internal bleeding. I'm so sorry, but we lost both her and the baby."

I collapse to my knees, my stomach constricts as waves of nausea take over. My breathing starts to increase as sweat builds on the back of my neck ...

I wake up clutching my chest and gasping for air. *Fuck, it was just a dream.* Thank God. I haven't had that dream in over a decade. It's been that long since I lost Abigail and our unborn child. I remember the day she told me she was expecting and how excited we both were. Call it being young and dumb, or whatever you want, but we were both ecstatic. I wish now more than ever I could feel that same way with Cara, but how can I when what I created is putting her life at risk?

I vividly remember leaving Abigail to go to work. She was tired and going to sleep in, maybe skip classes for the day. And then the call came and she was gone. Everything happened so fast and since that day I haven't been the same person I once was. That is until I met Cara. For years, I've done a damn good job at blocking out every memory and detail possible. Since losing her, I've unattached myself from women and have used them for one thing and one thing only. But when Cara came into my life with her smart mouth and confidence, she spun my entire world upside down. *Damn it, why didn't I use protection?* I could kick myself right now. Since Abigail passed, I've always been a Nazi about it. Yet Cara clouded my judgment with the craving she brewed inside of me for her it had grown to be so immense that I had to feel her — all of her. I never thought about the consequences or questioned what we were doing. I couldn't have ever imagined anything like this would happen to me. Not again anyways.

I glance at the clock; it's six in the morning. Reaching for my cell phone, I notice the half-drunk bottle of Patrón on the table. Damn, that's why I slept through the night. I unlock my cell phone and there are a few missed phone calls — two from Cara and one from Vincent. I go into the text messages next and my heart breaks as I read Cara's words.

I really think we need to talk about this. I'm in just as much shock as you are. I understand that you need some space and as much as that kills me, I'll do my best to give it to you. But PLEASE don't turn your back on me. We did this together.

Motherfucker, why did this fucking have to happen? Everything between us was great; I felt so complete. Damn it, now we're both hurting. Unsure of what to do, I check the next text. It's from Vincent.

What the fuck happened? You need to call me.

I immediately call him, and he answers on the second ring, "Hey, how ya holding up, buddy?"

"Fuck, Vince. Where do I even begin?"

"Well, you can answer my question. How are you?"

"How do you think I am? I'm not good. How much do you know?"

"At first I didn't know anything. Lex left work saying Cara had called and she could barely understand what she was saying on the phone and was sick. I didn't think much of it at the time, but Lex called me late last night to say she wasn't coming home and explained everything."

"Did you tell anyone else?" I ask in a sharp tone.

"NO! Of course not. It's not my place to tell. What are you going to do?"

"Fuck, I don't know."

"You're not saying much this morning. What can I do to help?"

"You can take me back to the first time Cara and I slept together and make me pull my head out of my ass. I don't know why I was being so naïve. You would think I learned my lesson with Abigail."

"Is that what's got you so upset?"

"Yeah. That and the fact I'm not father material. Have you forgotten I'm covered in tattoos? How can I make any child proud? Then you add my line of work and that I'm gone for three to four straight days per week. This is all a clusterfuck of a mess."

"Are you drunk?"

"Not anymore."

"First of all, knock it off with the booze. Second, kids don't see tattoos; they see their parent. And you need to look at the positives with your work. You have an awesome, well-paying job, not to mention that you're home for three to four full days a week as well. Most parents can't say that."

"Don't call me a parent. I told you I don't know the first thing about this shit."

"Did you even listen to a word I just said? You did this, whether you like it or not."

"Yeah, I fucking heard you. And do you remember what happened the last time this occurred? Both Abigail and the baby died. Who's to say it's not because of me? Think about it — there has got to be something wrong with me."

"I'm trying to talk some sense into you. Do you remember when I was freaking out about asking Lex to marry me and you said, 'She's not Angela?' You need to take a dose of your own advice."

"Dude, that's way fucking different. I'm not talking about some bullshit with an ex who cheated on me. I'm talking life and death!" I scream into my phone and hang up.

Damn it!

I thought he would help me, not make this shit worse. I hop up unable to sit here and think any longer. I don't know what to do, but I have to get my mind busy. I stare at the bottle and as tempting as the Patrón is, I can't. I have to cover at the other station or Tom will have my head on a silver platter.

Maybe a shower will help. I walk into the bathroom and the sight of Cara's things hits me and hits me hard. *What the fuck have I done?* Why was I so idiotic to let this happen? My mind gets away from me, picturing her showering with a huge, round stomach. Water cascades down her precious, pink body that's filled with life, a life we created.

Being a little bitch, I run my hands over my face and

through my hair, pulling on the roots and screaming in anger. I'm losing my fucking mind.

I turn away from the image and my back on Cara because I'm a coward. She and that baby are better off without me. I'm no good for either of them.

I snatch my keys and bolt, heading out of my loft and taking the stairs down all eighteen flights, hoping that running the stairs will occupy my mind long enough to take a sliver of the pain away. I emerge into the lobby and head out the front doors, just as the sun is just beginning to rise.

I jump in my truck and drive, unsure of my destination, focusing on the road ahead of me. The stoplight changes from yellow to red and I gas it, running through the intersection like an asshole. Why do I feel the need to push the limits? I guess I could blame the anger; at this moment all I can see is red rage. Christ, it would feel amazing to hit something right now, whether with my truck or my fist. I don't have a preference.

I go to the only place that comforts me — my dad's. Pulling into the driveway, his house is quiet. I walk up and knock on the door. He opens it and I can barely bring my eyes to meet his. Moving out of the way, he gestures for me to come in. I give him a hug and walk over to the couch, flopping down and throwing my arm over my eyes.

"What's going on, Son?" he asks.

I shake my head back and forth, unable to speak the

words. He slaps my leg and I look up at him as he sits in the chair across from me. "Come on, you came here this early in the morning, so speak."

I sit up and rest my elbows on my knees. Leaning over, I stare at the carpet and shake my head again. "You were right, she *is* pregnant." That's all I say and I know immediately he gets what I'm going through. He and my mom picked me up ten years ago when I experienced this with Abigail. I know he knows what I'm facing.

"How does that make you feel?" he asks in a calm even tone.

"Like a fucking loser. What, was one girlfriend dying not enough? I've avoided relationships for this exact reason, and here I am about to ruin another life."

"Whoa, Son. I don't think I would go that far. First of all, you're not a loser. Maybe this happened for a reason and it's for the good, not to ruin either of your lives."

I rub my hands over my face and get off the couch. I can't sit here any longer. I start to pace thinking about his words. *Could this be for the good?* I find it hard to believe, not with my past. Plus, if things do work out, I'm no dad. I don't know the first thing about babies or which end is up when it comes to raising one.

My dad walks past me and into the kitchen. "Would you like a cup of coffee?" he asks.

"Nah. I have to get to work soon."

"What are you going to do about this? You can't just

avoid it, you know? You've done that for ten years."

"I don't know. I just need a little time to think."

"What does Cara have to say about this?"

I shrug my shoulders, ashamed that I left her. A man would've stayed around to stick this out. He would have comforted her and told her everything would be okay. But that's not me. I'm a pussy and run from my problems. It's what I do. It's the only way I know how to handle things, which is sad because it's not even handling them.

"Abel?" my father asks sternly, pulling me out of the irrational thoughts that consume me.

"I left when she told me."

"Son, you're not going to like this but I have to say it. You are just as responsible as she is for this whole situation. You cannot turn your back on her or that unborn child. Do you hear me, Abel Wesley?"

I nod my head and hug my father tightly as he embraces me. I look at the clock on the wall. It's 6:30. I have to get going if I don't want to be late for work. "Just promise me you'll do what's right?"

"I will," I say and turn away from the comfort of my dad's hold. I know I have to face this and can't avoid it forever. But I also have to find an answer within myself before I do so.

Chapter 22

Questioning

Pulling into the station, there are a few cars already here, including Troy's jeep and Matt's car. I park and hop out grabbing my bag. There is a breeze in the air and the flag is flying at half-staff. As much as I love my job, I hope I *never* die in a fire. I couldn't imagine being burned alive. I shake off the fear and walk in. The guys are quietly standing around chatting, I assume waiting for my order.

I introduce myself and learn who the other guys are and where they are helping out from. I notice that the truck and ambulance are filthy. Immediately I assign a group to pull them out and wash them. Troy follows me upstairs with another guy and I give them both assignments as well.

I set my bag down and get to work calling Tom, letting him know that we're here. I'm not sure what his expectations are for me covering, but I'm ready to find out. I want to keep myself distracted, and this is the time to do just that. While I talk to Tom, I shoot Vincent a quick e-mail apologizing for hanging up on him this morning.

Tom informs me that I'll be here for at least two weeks. He would like me to work them straight through, and inside I'm relieved to have the excuse that will help me avoid what's on my mind. I can tell right away that the guys are hard workers and the other stations sent me their best. Thankful that I didn't get the lazy bad seeds, I join them out front with cleaning the trucks.

Troy yells out to me that I have a phone call. "Who is it?" I ask.

"Your brother."

I'm relieved to hear it's not Cara and I go in to take the call. "What's up, dude?" I say, drying my hands.

"Hey, I just wanted to check on you. Are you doing okay?"

"I don't know. I'm just trying to stay busy. Have you talked to Lex? Is Cara okay?"

"Yeah, they're both good. She called the doctor and got some anti-nausea medicine for Cara. She's stopped throwing up, but she won't eat."

"Damn it. I shouldn't have asked. I can't do this right now, Vince. I appreciate you calling and all, but I need to focus on work. I'm really sorry. You have the number here. Call me if you need anything. Tom said I'll be here for at least two weeks."

"I understand. Hang in there, buddy."

"Thanks," I say hanging up.

I wake again from yet another nightmare; it's the same one I've been having. I walk to the kitchen and grab a bottle of water. I've been at the station for almost a week and I need to get away. I slide on my jeans and a t-shirt, texting Troy as I sneak out. I don't know where I'm headed, but I need to clear my mind, so I just drive, trying to focus on the road ahead of me. It's so early that there isn't any traffic.

I keep driving, unsure of my destination, that is, until I come up on a familiar area and automatically slow my truck. I begin to count, one … two … three … four … five … and I turn. There she is, and I slam on my brakes. Why I am here, God only knows. Looking over at the rows and rows of tombstones, my mother's sticks out to me like a lighthouse in the ocean.

I hesitantly open the door and step down to the ground. As my boots hit the pavement, I realize it's a cool crisp morning. I hadn't noticed earlier, so I grab a hoodie out of the back and walk over to the beautiful, black marble, heart-shaped stone. It is etched just as I remember it from the last time I was here.

Judith Ann Mileski, beautiful wife and mother. You will forever be missed.

I kiss the top of the cold stone, feeling a sting on my lips when they touch the cool granite, and I plop to the ground, completely defeated, lost, unsure, angry, and scared. Looking up to the cloudy sky, I close my eyes and start to talk to my mom.

Mom, I wish you were here to help me with this. I would give anything to talk to you again. I don't even know what to say. I take a breath and pull the hood up on my sweatshirt. I tuck my hands into the pockets and speak again. *I have a girlfriend. Or at least I did until last week. I fucked up again, and she's pregnant. It's not something that either of us planned and I don't know what to do.* I open my eyes and focus on the cracks in the cement. *Anyways, I know you can't speak to me, but if you could guide me and show me, I promise I'll listen. I know I don't know the first thing about kids, but please don't take them from me. Not like what happened with Abigail. I don't think I can survive that again. Besides, things with Cara are different. I love her, I really do.*

I take my sleeve and wipe my eyes. *Please just give me a sign. I'll do anything.* Standing up, I kiss her tombstone again and say goodbye. Walking away from where my mom rests peacefully, I feel a calmness and hold onto that feeling hoping it will stick with me.

Chapter 23

Regret

Troy offers me some lunch but I decline. I'm not hungry. How can I eat? My stomach is in knots and has been since I left Cara. Eating has been almost unbearable. "Dude. Are you okay? You've been really quiet this week."

I look up at him, realizing that I didn't even make eye contact when he offered me food. "Yeah, man, I'm good."

"You sure?"

"Uh huh. Hey, would you mind if I ran home real quick?"

"Sure, thing. Take your time."

"Thanks, bro."

I get up and leave without saying another word to the guys. Troy has become my right hand man and I trust him entirely. I know he can cover for me and I don't need to explain anything. I need to feed Puss anyways and I have to take a few moments to myself. The drive to my house is reasonably quick. Not as quick as from my station but at least it's still in town.

I park on the street rather than dealing with the garage and walk inside the lobby, catching the elevator up with a young couple. Their floor is first, and I find I'm getting anxious waiting to exit. Finally, as the elevator opens, I burst out and head down the hall. I open the door and step into my loft pressing my back against it as it closes. Suddenly my throat tightens and my breathing speeds up. *She's been here.* I can smell her. It's so strong that there's no denying it.

My eyes dart from one side of the loft to the other looking for any sign of her. Then I notice that Puss is going to town on a plate full of wet food. She must have stopped by and fed her. I check both the dry food and water. They're full.

I take another deep breath letting in her sweet scent, so sultry, a mix of vanilla and orchids.

I pull my phone out of my pocket and there's a missed phone call from her, but no voice mail. I take a moment contemplating calling her. I need to talk to Tom about a day off so she and I can actually talk about *everything*, then I'll call her. I pet Puss and then grab some more clothes before I leave my loft, heading out into the late afternoon. The sun is going down and I can't even remember where the day has gone.

Pulling away, my cell phone rings. I look at the

screen and it's Troy. "Hey, what's up, buddy?"

All I can hear is sirens in the background and I know they're on a call. *Sonofabitch.* "We just got dispatched to a motor vehicle accident off of eighty-five. Can you meet us there?"

"Yeah, of course. What's the cross street, and how many vehicles?"

"Chenango Drive. I'm not sure. It was called in by an eyewitness as a multi-vehicle accident."

Horns blare, and for the first time, it hurts my ears. "I'll meet you there."

I hang the phone up and hit the gas, driving as fast as I can. I know right where this accident is located and I'm trying to picture the layout of the streets. Eighty-five runs two lanes in each direction, and Chenango is just one lane in each direction. I wish I had a scanner or some form of communication to know what the hell is going on. As I approach the scene, I see the lights and know the guys made it here before me.

Traffic is blocked and I pull off on the shoulder and drive towards the chaos. When I pull up, I see two cars — a black SUV with severe front end damage and a small, red Volkswagen Beetle that's mutilated. I park next to the fire truck and run over to the black SUV. There's a middle aged female passenger who's being attended to by one of the rookies that's helping out from another station.

I cut in and assist him. "Ma'am, my name is Abel.

I'm a firefighter. Can you tell me where you're in pain?"

She reaches for her neck and blood is running down her temple; she must have hit it on the window. I don't have gloves yet, so I shouldn't touch her, but my instincts take over and my hands move to the sides of her head to brace her from moving. "Go grab a neck brace," I yell to the rookie.

"Just stay still, ma'am. You're going to be okay." I glance over at Matt as he is hard at work with an EMT on the driver. They remove him onto a stretcher and then wheel him away. He didn't look responsive at all. As they move, I watch Matt do chest compressions on him, straddling the patient on the gurney, which is never a good sign.

My eyes glance to the back and I see an empty car seat. Thank God their child is *not* with them. My mind is inundated with images of this being us — Cara, myself, and our child. All it takes is a split second for a tragedy to turn your world upside down. I experienced it once, and I'll be damned if I let anything happen to them now. The rookie comes back over with the brace and I get it on her neck. She is blinking heavily and I'm unsure if it's shock or if there is an underlying trauma issue. Matt comes over to us and I hear Troy yelling. I can't see him as I move towards his voice. But then I spot him, down an embankment with another car.

All I hear are the slowest words ever. "Jaws of life." Looking at the car, I feel the color drain from my face. I gasp for air and use every ounce of my strength to just stand, as I stare at the grey Audi.

No, no, no, no, no. Please don't let that be her.

My body moves automatically and I run like I've never run before. Getting closer, I see Troy's face as he struggles to get the door open. Before I reach the car, I slow. Tears are welled up in my eyes, as I find the will to speak the words. "Is it her?"

He nods his head and I collapse. Screaming, "No! Damn it, no!"

"Is she …?" I can't get the words out as I begin to dry heave. I'm terrified of what I might see. Her fucking car is mangled; it has clearly flipped God only knows how many times. I couldn't imagine the impact she went through to end up down here.

"She's barely conscious, Abel. I really need you right now," he yells.

I nod my head and know what I have to do as I jog over to her car. Sure enough it's Cara and she is almost unrecognizable. I am utterly stunned by what I'm looking at. Blood and bruises cover just about every visible part of her. Her once platinum blonde hair, is now stained red with blood. She has her head slumped to the side and her eyes are closed. "Let me try," I tell Troy.

I pull on the door, but it's not budging. Matt comes over with the Jaws of Life and I move out of the way. Instinctively I try to open the other car doors. Finally the passenger door opens and I climb in. The car is squished so I can barely get to her. But once I do, I gently touch her. "Baby, I'm here with you. Can you hear me?"

She tries to lift her head a little, but that's all she manages. There are no words or sounds that come out of her. "You're going to be okay, kitten. Just hang in there for me, okay? " I reach for her hand and place it in mine. On her wrist is the infinity bracelet. My heart wrenches at the sight of my eternal gift wrapped around her delicate wrist. What was once pure gold is now spattered with blood. I regret not giving it to her myself. However, seeing it on her wrist shows me she hasn't given up on me, or us. She feels lifeless and that scares the shit out of me. I press her hand to my lips and hold it against my face. Having her in my hold completes me. I realize now how much of an asshole I've been. I never should've walked out on her. The guys are working as hard as they can to get her side of the car accessible. Removing her through the passenger side would be too risky.

"Please, baby, hang in there. I love you." Tears run down my face and I wipe them away on the shoulder of my shirt. The guys finally get her door open and I set her hand back in her lap. Sprinting around the car to help them get her out, I say to them, "Please be careful with her, she's pregnant."

"Okay, Chief," Matt says.

We delicately remove her from the car, following all safety measures to a T. Once she is on the body-board, I notice she's wearing my favorite sweats. Matt and I strap her securely down as Troy slides a neck brace around her, and then moves the last strap over her forehead. We all lift her on the count of three and head towards the waiting ambulance.

"How far along is she?" Troy asks.

"I'm not sure, we just found out last week."

Troy fills in the EMT while I get into the back of the ambulance. It takes everything I have not to start working on her. Instead, I keep out of the way and ensure I'm touching and talking to her at all times.

Within seconds, we're driving off. I don't recognize the EMT, but as I watch him, I can tell he knows what he's doing.

"Where are we taking her?" I ask.

"Good Samaritan."

In a way, I'm relieved that it's not her hospital. Then again maybe that would be better. The staff all knows who she is, so they would make her their top priority. But now is not the time to start questioning her care.

"What's the extent of her injuries so far?"

"I'm not sure, as there's not much physical trauma besides that to her head. She's going to need an MRI. Her BP is low, 50/80 so that's concerning to me. The firefighter I spoke with said she's pregnant."

"Yeah. We just found out."

"Alright, we're here. Let's let the experts take over." The ambulance slows and the back doors open. I hop out and have to remind myself to keep out of the way.

Waiting for us is a young nurse that reminds me of Cara and a doctor. Reading his nametag, it says Dr. Lee.

We all head inside and I do my best to keep up with the conversation that is going on between the three of them. I can tell they are taking her away for an MRI. She is stable enough for it, and their main concern is her head trauma. That seems to be where the bulk of her injuries are.

"Will you please check on the baby?" I say as a nurse stops me from following them as they wheel her away. Dr. Lee looks back to me and nods his head. I stand there in the stark, white hallway, frozen as I watch the reason for my existence be taken away from me. Emotions roll through me, and I have to get a breath of fresh air.

Once I'm outside, the air is a welcome feeling. The worry and anxiety from knowing that Cara is pregnant to the very real fear for her life has my throat constricting and each breath is a struggle. It's been a long time since I've had a full-fledged panic attack and I can feel one building now. I fight with my breathing and pray that it will go away.

I wish more than anything that I could go back to last week, waking up before Cara and watching her sleep ever so peacefully. If only I could switch places with her now, I would.

Leaning against the rough exterior of the side of the building, I know I have to call Lex. But what do I say? I can't imagine that phone call, so instead like a bitch, I call my brother. He answers on the second ring like he always does.

"What's up, douchebag?"

I swallow hard and push away the emotions in my voice. "Not now, Vince. Listen, it's Cara." I can't control the tone of my voice as I get choked up.

"What happened?" he demands.

"She … she was in a car accident," I can barely get the words out as my body skids down the wall. I sit there hanging my head low, quietly releasing my tears.

"Is she okay?"

"She's alive, but I don't know about the baby or the extent of her injuries yet."

"Where are you? We're leaving now."

"At Good Samaritan."

"Hang in there, okay? Please don't think the worst. She's alive and in good hands."

"I know," is all I can say and I hang up. I drop my phone and rest my head on my forearm, saying a silent prayer. Then it hits me — is this the sign from my Mom that I was asking for? Would she do that? Would she put Cara at risk to show me what I am supposed to be doing? Regardless, I've made my mind up.

I love her. Almost losing her is the biggest wake-up call ever. She completes me and is my reason for living. She's *not* Abigail, this I know. That was over a decade ago, and I have to let it go. She is Cara, my Cara. My kitten and my love, the mother of my child, and I need to not take her for granted.

Before I get up, I say another prayer. *God, please don't take her. Let her pull through this and be okay. Protect the little life that's inside of her as well.*

Walking back inside, my mind drifts. I know I don't know the first thing about being a parent, but I promise I'll give them both nothing less than 100%. I head back into the ER and sneak back with another visitor. I stop at the nurses' station to see if there are any updates. There is nothing new, and she tells me to have a seat, so I sit down in the waiting area. Leaning forward, I rest my elbows on my knees and bow my head.

I'm not sure how long I have been sitting like this. A gentle touch to my back alerts me and I look to my left. Alexa is sitting next to me, with tears in her eyes. I look up and see Vincent standing on the other side of me. Alexa leans over and hugs me, sobbing into my shoulder.

"How is she?" Vincent asks as he sits.

"I haven't heard anything yet."

Holding Alexa makes me realize how real this situation is. Cara is anything but out of danger. Vincent pats my shoulder as we all three sit in silence. The only noise is that of Alexa sniffling, and all we can do is sit and wait.

"Do you have Amber's number?" I ask.

As Alexa pulls away, she grabs a tissue off of the table and wipes her eyes before saying, "I called and left both her and Marla a message, I'm sure they'll call me soon. Abel, what happened?"

"I really don't know," I say running my hands over my face. "I ran home to get away for a bit and check on Puss, and the next thing I know I got a call from one of the guys that we had been dispatched. When I arrived I only saw two cars on the road, and neither were hers. Troy spotted her off the road and called me over … now here we are."

"What happened to her car? Did she just veer off of the road?"

I shake my head. "No. It flipped quite a few times. She was stuck inside and barely conscious. It took the guys awhile to get her out. I'm not sure if she knew I was there or not and that scares me. It seems as though her only injuries are head trauma, which I guess is better for the baby. But we don't know how bad it is for her yet."

Alexa starts to cry again and I wrap my arm around her pulling her against me.

"Cara Savannah," Dr. Lee comes into the waiting room and calls. We all stand and he comes over to us. "Please have a seat," he says.

I grip onto Alexa and neither of us moves. "How is she?" I ask.

"She has a long road ahead of her. There is severe trauma and swelling to her brain. We have her sedated and need to wait for the swelling to decrease before we can try to wake her. Other than several bumps and bruises, she doesn't have any other injuries. All in all, I would say she's very lucky."

"And the baby?" Alexa asks.

"The baby is fine. She appears to be about six weeks pregnant."

"Thank God. Can we see her?"

"Yes. It's important that you talk to her and let her know that you are there. Don't talk as if she's not in the room; include her in everything you all discuss. Studies have shown that patients who are in comas or sedated respond better to treatment when they are interacted with."

"Thank you," I say.

"This is what we do; it's my pleasure. Follow me, guys."

We all walk behind him and my heart is in my throat. It's the same feeling I got the first night that we slept together. When I drove to her house that night, unsure if she was okay, and walked up to her front door questioning everything ... then as she opened the door in her sweats, with her messy hair, and was excited to see me, my heart calmed.

Entering her room now, I don't get that same calmness. But she is alive. One thing about Cara is she's resilient. I see that strength in her now. Her beauty is still ever-present, as she shines through the bruises and bandages. I wish this were a dream that I could wake up from. But I know I can't, this isn't a fairy tale. This is our life and I am going to fight for her and our child.

I move to the right side of the bed and enclose my hand over her fragile one. Moving my lips to hers, I breathe her in. I can barely make out her sweet scent over the sterile stench of the hospital and that makes my heart wrench.

Thank you, Lord, for saving them.

I move my other hand and rest it on her abdomen; the simple touch brings me to my knees. Inside of her is a life that we created, a tiny seed with the slightest flutter of a heartbeat. A tough one, might I add. Jesus, I never knew I could feel so deeply for something I ran away from just a week ago. I know it has not been long but to me it feels like months and months. How will we get through this? What if she doesn't wake up? *Mom, if you have any pull in this, I could really use a saving grace right about now.* I rest my head against my forearm, looking for the strength to speak to her.

Alexa's voice interrupts my thoughts. I look, and both she and Vincent are on the other side of the bed. Alexa takes the back of her knuckles and runs them over Cara's swollen cheek. Her poor face is bloody and bandaged. "Care, it's Lex. I'm here with the guys and we're not going to leave your side. The doctor said that the baby is okay. You guys are six weeks pregnant and I think Abel is happy."

She looks to me as I stand. I need to be a man and tell her how I feel.

Please let her hear me.

"We'll give you some time," Vincent says as he directs Alexa away.

"I'll be right back," she adds.

Once the door closes, I lean over inches from her face and wish that she would open her eyes. I move my lips to hers and then to my favorite spot behind her ear, the one that drives her a little crazy. After I leave a tender kiss I begin to speak into her ear.

"Baby, I love you. I need you to know that. I'm sorry I didn't tell you sooner. I was afraid of your reaction. Quite frankly, it doesn't matter though. I can't change how I feel for you. I love you with every fiber of my being and have for a long time. All I can do now is hope you'll love me in return. I'm so sorry I left you. It was a shitty thing to do, and if you can forgive me, I promise to *never* do anything like that again. I was being dumb and immature. I panicked and should've talked through my feelings with you."

I pull up a chair and sit in it, feeling exhausted. I lower the railing on the bed and rest my head on her side as I continue to talk. "I promise you I'll be open and honest from now on. I know I don't know the first thing about being a father, but I'm going to give it my all. I won't let you or this little one down."

Moving my hand to rest on her stomach, I feel tired and allow myself to close my eyes for a few moments. I relax there with my eyes shut, her breathing moving my hand up and down. I can feel her heartbeat pulsing through her and it's strong. She's going to be okay; she has to be. God forbid something happens to her — I wouldn't survive it. I couldn't imagine life without her.

Chapter 24

Pebble

These last two weeks have been hell. Every day is the same; I wait for things to change but nothing does. The swelling has gone down in Cara's brain and they weaned her off of the sedation a week ago. Since then she has been in a coma. Her brain is responsive and showing normal activity, but she's just not waking up.

I've spent hours upon hours researching similar cases. I finally had to stop; the information was driving me crazy. Dr. Lee said she just needs a little more time and that's what I keep reminding myself of. Trauma patients often wake up when their bodies have healed enough or when their minds have been able to process the trauma it's endured. Marla and Amber arrived a few days after the accident. I feel horrible that they had to find out about the baby through this hospitalization. They've both been huge supporters though, even Marla with her kooky ways. It's taken a bit of adjusting on my part to have them around. Regardless, I'm happy to have their support.

Staring at the eclectic selection of items in the gift shop, I try to enjoy a moment alone. It's the first I've taken away from her in a few days. Everyone demanded I do so and I finally got tired of arguing. Looking around, I snag a few sports magazines then scan the shelves looking for anything interesting. I find a small scroll attached to a pebble. As I open the scroll it says,

In life, it is said that each person has one true mate. The same holds true for penguins. They spend years searching for their perfect match. Once they've found their mate, the male will present the female with a perfect pebble. He places it at her feet as a sign of his everlasting commitment. If she accepts, these two are united for all eternity.

I know penguins are Cara's favorite animal. She would love this, and I hope I get the chance to present it to her. I cash out and head into the cafeteria. Grabbing a tuna sandwich, some chips, and a soda, I take my lunch to her room because I can't stand being away from her any longer.

As I approach, there is chaos and I jog over to see what is going on. Dr. Lee and the neurologist, Dr. Cottingham, are checking on her. She looks the same — pale and small — in the large bed.

"What happened?" I ask Amber.

"My mom and I were talking about you and she squeezed my hand."

"Really?" I say way too loudly in my excitement. She nods her head. "Is she waking up?" I ask Dr. Cottingham.

"It's hard to tell. A lot of times similar patients will seem to be responding, but it's just their reflexes. Abel, if her response was truly to her hearing Amber and her mom talk about you, then I think you're going to be the one to pull her out of this. She's stable and everything looks good, so I'll leave you to it and be back in a few hours."

"How's the baby?" I ask.

"The baby's fine. Stop worrying," he says and pats my shoulder as he walks off. I go back over to Cara, and notice that her lips look dry. I grab her chapstick and put a thin layer on her plump, pink lips. Then of course I lean down and kiss them. Man, what I wouldn't give to have her kiss me back. I sit in my usual chair with Marla and Amber across from me.

I do what I've done so many times — I just talk to her. I talk about everything, from the news, to baby names, and even reminisce about the past and what the future might hold for us. As I speak, the hours pass like minutes and the sun is setting. Marla begins to yawn and Amber recommends they leave for the night. I hug them both and promise to call if there are any changes.

Once they leave and we're left alone, this is truly my favorite time. I dim the lights and pull the covers back at her feet. The nurses gave me permission to rub them. I turn off the blood pressure leg machine that inflates to help with circulation, remove my shoes, and get into bed with her.

I sit cross-legged resting her feet in my lap and rub her feet with some cherry almond lotion. We both love the scent; it's always been one of my favorites, more so now than ever. Watching intently while I massage, I'm looking for any signs of movement.

"Baby, I almost forgot to mention that I bought you something today. But I'm not going to tell you what it is until you're awake. For now, I'll hold onto it for you."

It's ironic that I'm rubbing her feet as I'm talking about the pebble. My eyelids start to get heavy and I know I need to rest as well. I put one last coat of lotion on her and then grab a clean pair of socks out of the closet. Once the socks are on, I place her legs back in the machine and turn it on. I cover her loosely like she likes and lay the bed all the way back.

I grab my blanket and pillow from the closet and get as comfortable as I can in my chair. While I lay there, I watch her small, even breaths. I can hear her laugh, and feel her arms around my neck.

Lord, please give me that again.

"Goodnight, kitten. I love you."

I rest my hand in hers and close my eyes. Exhaustion sets in quickly and I drift off to a peaceful sleep.

"Baby," she whispers and moves her hand beneath mine. I curse inside for having another one of these dreams, but it's the closest I've been to being with her, so I let myself indulge yet again.

"Abel," she says a little more loudly and then begins to cough. My head jerks up and I'm shocked. She's awake and really coughing. I run to the sink and fill her up a cup of water. I don't hand it to her though, as I'm unsure of her strength. I place my hand behind her head and give her a small sip. She swallows and looks up at me. "Thank you," she whispers in a small, raspy voice.

"Of course. I'm going to call a nurse."

She shakes her head, "No nurses, not yet. I need you."

I kiss her lips, "You have me."

"No, I don't. You left me," she says as tears fill her eyes.

"Oh, kitten," I say and climb into bed next to her, wrapping her delicate body against mine. I'm at a loss for words. I ... I don't even know where to begin.

"What happened?" she asks.

"You were in an accident, a few weeks ago. I got called on the scene, as well as Troy and Matt. Your car flipped quite a few times and they struggled to get you out. Since then you've been in a coma."

She places her hand over her mouth to stifle a cry, "Oh no, the baby."

Reassuringly, I rub her stomach. "The baby is fine.

You're about eight weeks along."

"Really?"

"Yes, baby, really. Cara, I want you to know how sorry I am for walking out on you. If I could go back and do things over, I *never* would've left you. It's the dumbest thing I've ever done, but I need you to know why. Over a decade ago, I had a girlfriend and she got pregnant. It was a tubal pregnancy and both she and the baby passed. That's why I've never wanted kids and I panicked when you told me about the baby. I was scared of losing you too. But I've realized that you're not her, plus our little one is strong."

"Jesus, Abel. I'm so sorry. I wish you would have told me this before."

"It's okay, baby. The important part is that you're okay. Do you remember anything from the accident or when you were out?"

She closes her eyes and is deep in thought. "I was driving home from your place. I just went to feed Puss and someone hit me. I think my car flipped, but that's all. Everything from that point on is like a dream"

"Do you remember me telling you that I love you?"

She looks at me with wide eyes and blinks a few times, "Yeah, I do. You said it in my car, but I thought I was dreaming."

"That was not a dream. I love you, Cara, more than anything in this world."

Tears fall from her eyes as she speaks, "Oh Abel, I love you too."

I never thought it would be so easy for us to say the words to one another, but it is. Leaning down I press my lips to hers, allowing the tears to escape my eyes as well. After weeks of praying for this, it's come true. Finally she is kissing me back. Our tears blend together and meld as if they are one. From this moment on, we are one ...

"Sir," an unfamiliar voice calls out. My eyes fly open and standing next to me is a nurse. "You really shouldn't be in bed with the patient."

"She's awake," I say.

The expression on the nurse's face changes and she moves to the other side of the bed. "Cara, can you hear me?" she asks.

But Cara doesn't respond. I lean down and kiss behind her ear, then say, "Kitten, you need to wake up."

She moans and blinks a few times. "See? She's awake," I say and slide out of bed.

"Cara. I'm Alice. How are you feeling?"

"I guess okay, considering," she says in a hoarse voice.

"Good. Let me page Dr. Lee. He needs to examine you."

Before the nurse leaves, she checks Cara's vitals, writing everything down on her chart. I can't keep my eyes off of her as she lies so quietly in bed. Her nipples are hard, making my mouth water. Fuck, I shouldn't be looking at her like this. Not now, she's too fragile, but I can't stop staring at them straining against the thin fabric of the hospital gown. I force myself to move my eyes from her breasts to her eyes. A grin is spread wide across her face, making me realize, she caught me and I'm the happiest man alive for it. She gets me and that's one of the things I love about her.

Patience is not something that comes easily to me, but I waited for Cara months ago and it was the best decision of my life. As much as my body is screaming for her now, needing to claim her and make love to her slowly, I'll wait however long is needed until she is healthy and strong enough to partake in our sweetest indulgence. I mouth the words I love you to her, and she returns them.

Dr. Lee conducts a thorough examination on Cara and all is well. The nurse removes all of her tubes and sends us on a walk. The short distance makes her tired and I know there is a long road ahead. Dr. Lee says she should be able to go home in a few days and I've never been happier.

Amber and Marla stop by briefly and then leave to get Cara's place ready for her homecoming. As much as I want to take her home to my loft, that will have to wait. For now she can stay in Alexa's old room if she needs to avoid the stairs.

Lex and Vince are with her now while I am at my place grabbing my stuff and visiting with little Puss. I haven't seen this little girl in so long, and I've missed her. "You know we are going to have to move and get a bigger place," I say. She meows and I laugh at myself for talking to a cat.

Neither my place nor Cara's is big enough for a baby. I wonder what her thoughts are going to be. We'll have to discuss it at a later time. All I know is that I'll be happy wherever the two of them are.

Leaving my place, I drive back to the hospital and enter the familiar halls I've unfortunately grown to know. Walking back into the room, Cara is fast asleep and Alexa's reading a magazine. I smile and before I sit I have to kiss Cara and as our lips touch, she smiles and looks at me. "Sorry I didn't mean to wake you."

"It's okay."

"How are you feeling?" I ask.

She nods her head, "Good, I think."

"You better be feeling good, you've slept the entire time I've been here," Alexa says.

We all laugh and Cara shrugs her shoulders. "Well, I do need to run, you two. I have to get back to the office and help Vince. He has a big case that he's prepping for. It goes to trial tomorrow, so I'm sure he's a wreck."

"Thanks for staying," I say to her.

"It was no problem. I enjoyed some time with Cara, and I guess she didn't sleep the entire time I was here."

She hugs us both and walks out of the room. Tilting my head to the side I look at Cara and soak in her beauty.

"What did you do while you were out?"

"I ran home and checked on Puss. She thinks we should move."

She laughs out loud and I love to hear it. "Really? What else did Puss say?"

"That's it. But she said it needs to happen before the baby is born."

"Abel, are you serious right now?"

"I'm dead serious, baby. Think about it. Neither of our places is big enough for a baby and unless you are leaving me, I'm in this for the long haul."

"Is that why you gave me this bracelet?" she asks, lifting her wrist and showing me her infinity bracelet.

"I didn't even get to give it to you. Take it off and let me do this right," I say.

She removes it and hands me the heavy gold symbol of our love. Grabbing her hand, I sit in bed next to her and swallow hard. "Cara, I'm giving you this bracelet as a symbol of my love. I bought it for you on the day I planned to tell you that I love you. I can't take back the past, or what has happened, but I can change the future. I want you to know from the bottom of my heart how much I love you. Thinking about our future and knowing we have a full life ahead of us makes me the most content I've ever been. For the first time in years, I'm satisfied. I'm no longer the shell of a man I once was. I see value within myself and that is all because of you."

"Oh, baby," she says crying and leans up wrapping

her arms around my neck. Holding her body, I breathe her in and thank God for this miracle. Once we separate, she watches me as I go to clasp the gold symbol back around her tiny wrist, but not before I ask, "Did you see the engraving?"

Looking at me confused, I point to the inside of the bracelet where I had the special message placed. She squints and reads the tiny writing out loud, "To my kitten, I love you more than life." She shakes her head back and forth in disbelief. "I can't believe you did that, it's perfect. Thank you so much, Abel."

Leaning down, I kiss her and lose myself in her soft lips. She tastes like paradise and I've never known a feeling like the one I have now. In her hold, being complete and content, I know I'm the luckiest man alive.

Chapter 25

Tesla

Cara came home this morning and is in really good spirits. She just woke from a nap and is nestled on the couch with me, cuddled in my lap. She's talking with her mom and Amber. I'm trying my best to listen in, but my mind keeps drifting. My phone vibrates on the coffee table and I reach for it. It's Vincent. *Can you sneak away today?*

Why would I do that? I just got them back.

Come on. I need your help with something for Cara. She has her mom and sister there to keep her company.

Do I really need to come with you?

Yes, you do and if you don't, I'll send Lex over there and make her kick your ass out for the day. Come on, it's for Cara.

Fine.

Cool, I'll pick you up in thirty.

I wait for a break in conversation before I tell her. Taking my hand I run my fingers over the tender skin of her arm. Goosebumps form on the surface, and she looks at me.

"Sorry."

She shakes her head, "It's okay."

I lean down once Marla and Amber are off in their own conversation. "Vince just texted me. He needs me to help him today."

She smiles and says, "Okay, baby."

"Are you sure?"

"Yeah, you haven't left my side in weeks. Go spend some time with your brother. It'll be good for you."

I kiss her perfect lips. "Thank you. I love you."

"I love you too."

I slide out from underneath her. "Ladies, I'm going to run and help my brother for a bit. I'll be back soon."

Marla stands and hugs me, "Take your time."

"Thanks," I respond and high five Amber. She's so goofy. She has such a free spirit like Cara.

I look in the mirror and decide against changing. Whatever he has planned, he can take me in my basketball shorts and a t-shirt. I grab a hat, put on a pair of tennis shoes, then I hear him honk out front. *Damn, that was fast.*

I go into the living room and grab my cell phone, placing a kiss on Cara's forehead and tummy. "Love you," I say and head for the door.

Vincent is parked out front in his Bugatti with the top down. As I get in, he's wearing grey dress slacks, and a white dress shirt with the sleeves rolled up. Okay, maybe I'm way underdressed for what he has in mind.

"How ya holding up, big papa?" he jokes, speeding off.

"I'm good. How's my douche of a brother?"

"I'm great."

"So what do you need my help with today?"

"I take it Lex didn't call you and spill the beans?"

"Dude, your lingo fucking sucks, who even says 'spill the beans?'"

"Fuck you. Who says 'lingo?'"

"Shut up! No, Lex didn't call me, should I call her?"

"No. Just relax, man, you're so edgy today. I told you I needed your help with this for Cara. Enjoy a few minutes away. She's fine. Lex is gonna swing by anyways with lunch in a bit. Plus we won't be too long."

"Sorry. I just hate leaving her. It puts me on edge. Last time I left her … well, you remember what happened."

"I know, but she's safe. You know you can't keep her in a bubble all the time. You both are going to go back to work next week."

"I know," I respond. Then I think about her going back to work, on her feet for twelve hours a day, dealing with sick patients, and putting herself and the baby at risk.

"How is she?" he asks.

"She's great. She's so resilient; I really admire her

strength. I hope the baby gets that from her."

"It's still weird to hear you talk about a baby."

"I know it is."

We're both quiet for the rest of the drive. I stare out at all of the sights and the people who are enjoying this summer day. It's not long before Vincent says, "We're here," turning into the lot of a Tesla dealership.

"No way. You're not buying her a car."

"The hell I'm not."

"There's no way she's going to accept it."

"Oh yes she will. I promised her a car if Lex said yes when I proposed. You know I'm a man of my word. Plus you have to admit these cars are sick. She's gonna love it."

"Dude, I can't let you do this."

"Yes, you can and you will. I wouldn't have brought you if I thought you were going to be such a pain in the ass. I'm making good on my debt. Plus, my nephew or niece needs the safest car available."

I shake my head and get out of the car, following my brother over to a row of sleek four-door sedans. A salesman greets us dressed in a navy suit with black wavy hair. *Man, I really am underdressed today.*

"Gentleman, I'm Raj. What brings you in today?"

"Nice to meet you, Raj. I'm Vincent, this is my brother, Abel." We both shake Raj's hand. "We need to buy a car for my sister-in-law," Vincent says. Hearing him use the term so casually catches me off guard.

"Perfect, will she be coming in as well to pick it out and do the paperwork?"

"No, it's a gift and I'll be paying cash. I was hoping I could put it in her and my brother's name?"

"Yes, sir, that's not a problem. Do you know which model?"

"I was thinking the four-door S. After researching, that seems to be the most practical and has the best safety features."

"The S is a great vehicle. Follow me this way; I'll show you what we have in stock. If there's something that we don't have we can always custom order it for you."

I walk behind them looking at the rows and rows of cars. Cara really does need a new car. I'm sure it will still be a few weeks before she sees any insurance money for hers. Plus, that'll just be enough for another used car. This will be brand new, top of the line, with the best safety features for her and the baby.

"What color do you think she'll like?" Vincent asks me.

"Oh, man. I honestly don't think she'll care. She's going to be so excited, it could be shit brown and she would love it."

Raj laughs. "Women seem to lean towards the white and silver colors. I have a white one right here. Surprisingly this one has black interior; most have white on white. It's a Tesla thing."

"Dude, it's gorgeous," I say.

"Can we test drive this one?" Vincent asks Raj.

"Sure, I'll just need a driver's license and I can grab the key." Raj takes Vincent's ID, and runs inside.

"Are you sure about this, Vince?"

He laughs at me and shakes his head. "Yes. Don't ask me again, or I'll buy you one too."

I lift both my hands up signaling defeat. "Are you sure about the white?" he asks me.

"Yeah. Her room is white, so I know she loves the color."

Raj hands Vincent the key, who tosses it to me and says, "You're driving."

I know better than to argue with him. Quite frankly, if my family is going to be in this car, I need to be comfortable with it as well. The three of us load up and Raj explains the bells and whistles of the interior. There's a touch screen on the display panel – it's huge! It's also an electric car, so no gas is required, which is awesome.

Pulling out onto the road, I notice the vehicle handles exceptionally well. It's smooth and easy to maneuver. "Raj, what if you need to charge the car while you're out during the day?" I ask.

"I'm glad you asked that. I was just going to mention that across the city, Tesla has multiple charging stations located at popular attractions. All of them are in their own special parking locations. You pull in, front row, plug in, and enjoy your day. But you shouldn't need to do that often; your battery will run for three hundred miles on a single charge. And we include an extra battery that can easily be exchanged if needed in less than three minutes."

Driving back to the dealership, Vincent asks me, "What do you think?"

"It's perfect. She's going to love it. Thank you, Vince."

"It's my pleasure. We'll take it, Raj."

"Awesome, I think your brother's wife will love it."

"Yes, yes, she will," Vincent says, not correcting Raj.

The paperwork is easy, I guess because there isn't much to be done. Cara just needs to stop by and sign her half. Then Vincent hands over his black AMEX card and we are on our way to Cara's. I can't wait to see the smile on her face when she sees her new car. Pulling up, Alexa's Porsche is in the driveway next to my truck. I guess that's my cue to park on the street. I do so and climb out just as Vincent greets me.

"Do you want me to get her?" I ask, handing him the key.

"Have her come to us." He leans in and presses the horn a few times. I see Amber look out the kitchen window and then the front door opens. My mouth turns into a smile at the sight of her. She is stunning, dressed in a white linen dress with a brown leather belt below her boobs. As she walks towards us, I swear she is starting to show a little bit.

"What the hell is this?" she asks me.

"Your new car," Vincent interjects and tosses her the key.

"Holy shit. No way."

She looks from my brother to me and wraps her arm around my waist. Shocked would be the best way I could describe the expression on her face. "Why?"

"Well, for starters, your car is totaled. And I told you I would buy you one. I'm just paying off my debt," he says.

She slaps his arm and he flinches away from her laughing. "That was a joke!" she yells.

"Oh, it was? Well, too late now. Enjoy your new car."

"I don't even know what to say."

"Don't say anything, baby. I already fought with Vincent about this. Accept his gift and let's take it for a test drive."

She lets go of my waist and hugs him. As she reaches her arms around his neck and presses herself against him, she is definitely showing. I can see the small bump pushing through her white dress. *This is really going to happen.*

Chapter 26

Forever

Waking up next to Cara is such a surreal feeling. I've dreamt of this so many times and since she is home, it still doesn't feel real. This morning I feel like a ball of nerves. I'm hoping to have all of that eased at her appointment today.

I know I've been overbearing but my mind keeps drifting back to my past with Abigail, and I'm terrified that something is going to happen to Cara and the baby. She has been so tired and that scares me. While I lie here and watch her sleep peacefully, I don't want to wake her, but I have to. She's a picture of perfection. Her lips are slightly parted, with her hair spread across her pillow. Her cheeks are red and I worry she has a fever. I lean down and kiss her cheek to cheek, but it's cool to my lips. A smile spans her face and she stretches. Nudging my head into her neck, I continue to bathe her with kisses to wake her.

She laughs a little and pushes me away. I look at her as she blinks a few times, trying to completely wake up. "That tickles," she grumbles.

I crease my eyebrows and run my hand over her neck to sooth the skin I just ravished with my mouth. "Better?" I ask.

She nods her head and I lay my head against her chest, listening to her heartbeat and breathing. "What time is it?" she asks.

"It's almost noon. I didn't want to wake you, but I don't want you to rush getting ready for your appointment."

"Thank you. I can't wait to see the baby today."

I take a deep breath thinking about what the day will hold. I know everything will be okay. It has to be. God wouldn't have given them back to me in turn to take them away. The appointment will go as planned and she will get the green light on her health and the baby's.

"Are you hungry?" I ask.

"Yeah."

"Why don't you get ready and I'll make you some breakfast?"

"Thanks, babe, that would be great."

I kiss her lips and then her belly before I hop off the bed and head out of the room. *Just give her some space.* I tell myself that, but it's not as easy. I force myself into the kitchen and pour another cup of coffee. Once I take a sip, I look in the cabinets and then fridge.

I decide on a bagel and some orange juice. Just when I push the toaster down, I notice a note on the counter from Amber. *I got Mom out of the house so you guys could enjoy your appointment in peace. Love ya.*

Geez, that girl has had my back. I really need to find a way to thank her. As I finish up Cara's breakfast, she comes out with her hair in a towel, dressed in a short summer dress.

She sits on the bar stool to eat and I can't help but watch her, even though I know it drives her crazy. "I'm going to change while you eat, then we can hit the road. Okay?"

She nods her head yes with a mouth full of bagel and I can't help myself from wiping the cream cheese off of the corner of her lips. She watches as I lick it off of my thumb and then walk away. Just touching her mouth like that gets my dick hard. I don't know how much longer I can last without being inside her.

On the drive across town for her follow up appointment, both of us are extremely quiet. I know for me it's because I'm nervous. I hope she's not experiencing the same fears and anxiety as I am. All either of us can do at this point is pray. As we park and head in, I wrap my arm around her waist pulling her close against me. Deep down, I know everything will be okay, it has to be …

Brushing my teeth, I watch Cara in the reflection of the mirror. She is glowing and finally looks back to her old self. After her appointment the other day, I finally feel a bit calmer although it has been unusual to adjust to no longer worrying. For me it's like I can't process that she and the baby are both actually okay. I find myself still hovering and still being overbearing when I know deep down I shouldn't.

"How are you feeling?" I ask.

She glares up at me from her iPad, "You know that's the twelve-hundredth time you've asked me today."

I rub the back of my neck thinking about her statement. "I don't know if I would say twelve hundred. Maybe a thousand, give or take a hundred."

She laughs at me and sets her iPad on the nightstand. "Are you going to get in bed with me?" she asks.

"I don't know if that's a good idea." I look down at my erection straining against my sweatpants.

"Oh," she says. "Well, it seems like we need to handle that."

"No, really, it's fine. I don't want to hurt you."

She points her finger at me and asks that I come to her. I oblige and sit next to her, trying to keep as much distance at I can. "You're not going to hurt me. Remember what the doctor said? It's completely safe for us to have sex. He said he saw no reason to wait and that was a few days ago. So, you either fuck me or I demand that you let me suck you off."

"Cara, I don't want to fuck you. I want to make love to you. I need to gently claim your pussy, and tell you that I love you while I'm doing it. I'll never fuck you again. Even if we get rough, I'll always be making love to you from this day forward."

"Then please make love to me, Abel."

There's no possible way I could ever say no to her. I remove the covers, exposing her body; again she in my sweats and one of my t-shirts. My cock begins to throb in anticipation. I cannot wait to devour her. Cautiously, I grab her hips and pull her down to the middle of the bed, placing her right where I want her to be. Tucking my hands under the waistband, I remove her pants; immediately she intoxicates me. Her pussy is so wet I can smell it, and I press my lips against the inside of each of her thighs with relish, leaving small kisses.

Kissing my way up her stomach, I spend an extra moment there and whisper to the baby. I take more time than usual with my hands, exploring her perfect body, and for a moment I imagine what she will look like nine months pregnant. Radiant and happy, carrying our unborn child. Gingerly she sits up and I lift the shirt above her head.

She lies back down and all I can do is just stare. She is perfect — the blondest hair, greenest eyes, and most flawless skin. Her breasts are still perky even when she is on her back. I take a handful of each and straddle her, swirling my tongue over each sensitive bud, just how she likes. I grasp each one in between my lips and tug. This causes her body to bow off of the bed and a moan escapes those luscious pink lips.

I tangle my fingers in her hair and claim her mouth. When I do so, her jaw is lax and she lets me control her. I slide my tongue inside and tease hers. My body is surging with eagerness. I cannot wait to enter her tight pussy and love her body with mine. *It's been so long.* She grabs my dick, taking me by surprise, and I groan loudly as we kiss.

Twisting her hand up and down, she works me till I'm about to burst. I have to pull away and rest my forehead against hers. She knows damn well what she's doing to me, as she lies there naked with a smile on her face. I take my hand and separate her wet, swollen pussy lips and get to work, rubbing her clit in a circular motion and then dipping a finger inside of her. *Fuck, she's wet for me.* I have to remind myself to keep things slow as I pull my finger in and out of her, touching her clit with my thumb every chance I get. Her body squirms beneath me and she quietly whimpers. "Do you want to come, baby?" I ask.

She nods her head.

"Tell me how much you love me then."

She whips her head back and forth as I continue to torture her, trying to compose herself enough to speak. "I love you more than anything. I love you more than —" She stops speaking and lets go. Her eyes are shut tightly and I watch her body shudder under my control, making sure I keep a steady rhythm, pulling out every last drop of her orgasm.

I look down at my finger still inside of her tender core. As she looks at me, all I see is love. She is so sexy after she comes. I pull my finger out of her and bring it to my mouth, pampering myself with her sweet taste. Pulling my finger out of my mouth, she stares at me and says, "You're so dirty."

I brace my weight above her, hovering inches from her face. "I'm not dirty. I love your pussy and I've been deprived of her. I can't help myself."

She pulls me down to kiss her. I plunge my tongue into her mouth; I'm so turned on I can barely control myself. She moves her hands and guides my pants down my ass. I kick them off and rub my cock against her clit.

Running her hands up and down my back, she kisses me like the first night we had sex. Stroking myself against her, I can tell she wants me. But before I enter her, there's something I need to do. Something I've been waiting to do.

I pull away and she looks at me confused. I take a deep breath and open my dresser drawer. Inside tucked under my clothes is her pebble, the perfect pebble for my perfect mate. I place it in my hand and lie back down on top of her.

"Before we make love. I have something for you." Feeling nervous, I swallow hard and kiss her behind her ear. "I bought this for you while you were in the hospital, and I wanted to give it to you at the perfect time." I place the small, glossy pebble on her chest. "That time is now. Before I enter your body, I want you to know that this will be forever for me. I'm giving you this as a sign of my eternal commitment to you and only you. Cara, I know I told you I love you, but those are just words. I want you to know what I truly feel for you. You're my soul mate, my one true love, and the mother of my child. I promise to love you unconditionally for the rest of our lives. The future is uncertain — we both learned that a few weeks ago. I don't want another day to pass us by where we don't live it to the fullest. I promise I will do everything in my power to make you the happiest woman alive."

As tears run over the sides of her eyes, she brings the pebble to her lips and kisses it. "I don't know what to say to that, except I want all of that and more. I didn't know I could love someone as much as I love you. You're right — the future is uncertain, so all we can do is enjoy every day together. Soon enough it won't just be the two of us, there will be three, and I've never been more excited about anything in all my life."

Holding her face in the palms of my hands, I slide

myself inside of her. Taking my time, as I watch her eyes and how they contract to me entering her body. It has to be the most beautiful thing I've ever seen. She wraps her arms and legs around my body and I feel the pebble in her hand, as she presses it against my back.

Slowly I begin to move, pushing myself in and out, the walls of her pussy tighten as she clings to me. Small, sweet cries of pleasure escape her beautiful mouth as I work, and they push me close to coming as well — her noises, coupled with the fact I haven't in weeks.

My movements are strong, yet gentle. Our legs become entangled as I hang on by a thread. Every thrust I swear will be the last before I explode, but it's not. I continue to move, until she comes again and whispers those words. The ones I was once so afraid of. Now I can't get enough of them. My balls constrict and I explode inside of her body. God, I love this woman. It takes everything I have to keep my composure and not scream like an animal. The havoc she wreaks on my body is ultimately my greatest pleasure.

Lying down on top of her, I wrap her tightly in my hold. My lips touch hers and I can't stop myself from kissing her over and over. I'm not using my tongue, just my lips and it's remarkable how good something so small feels. Once I pull out of her, I stretch my body along hers and tuck one arm underneath the pillow and the other across her belly. Holding her close, we both lie there in silence, neither of us moving, just the sound of our breathing, while our minds unravel. This is truly the happiest I've *ever* been.

Epilogue

Cara had to go into the hospital for a meeting this morning and I can't wait to see her and show her what I found today. Since it's my only day off from the station for the next few, I'm parked out front of her work waiting. I dropped her off earlier and had too much time on my hands to meander. I really didn't plan on doing this today, but I know Cara won't mind. She's always more than understanding, which is why I know she'll love it. Even though she's only been gone a few hours, I'm anxious to see her. Just then my phone chimes with a text from her.

I'm on my way, baby. Do you need anything?

Just you.

God, I love you.

Placing my phone in the cup holder, I wait for her to come out. Once she does, I smile at the sight of her. I'm in her sleek, white Tesla and as she approaches, she leans down into the passenger window and says, "Hi, baby."

"Hey, kitten. How was your meeting?"

"It was good," she says opening the door and sliding into the soft, black leather. She leans over meeting me in the middle, placing her hand on the back of my neck, kissing me.

"I have something I want to show you," I say.

"Baby, I'm all yours. Lead the way."

She places her seat belt below her tiny belly and we drive away from the hospital. On the drive, I wonder if she is curious as to where we are headed, but I let the anticipation build.

"Where are we going?" she asks.

"Patience, kitten, it's not too much longer."

Turning on her iPod, I listen to the words of a song I've never heard. Tears fill my eyes as the song ends and she looks at me. "That's my new favorite," she says.

"Who is it?" I ask.

"It's called 'Small Bump' by Ed Sheeran."

"It's just crazy to think that there is a tiny baby growing inside of you. It's half of each of us. I mean, we created it."

"It *is* crazy. I can't wait 'til we can feel the baby move."

"I know, me too."

I take a turn onto the wrong road. But being a man, I don't admit it. I just keep driving. We keep weaving more and more through the different neighborhoods. "Do you know where we are?" she asks.

"Of course."

"These houses are cute. Maybe we should look in this neighborhood," she says.

"Yeah, I agree. It seems like there are a lot of kids and young couples."

"Look, that one's for sale," she says.

Bingo. She nailed it.

I park in front of it and she looks at me. "What are you doing?"

"This is what I wanted to show you. It's an open house. Let's go inside and look."

I don't give her a second to answer. I hop out and walk around, opening her door and holding my hand out to her. "Come on, baby." She takes my hand and steps out. We both stand and stare at the two-story, grey and navy home. I love how dark it is. The exterior is modern yet colonial. We walk up the center stone pathway that is surrounded by plush, green grass.

The porch is long with a swing and I imagine many years out here with her. Before we can knock or open the door, the realtor does. "Hi, welcome," she says. "Please come in."

We enter and I'm blown away by the interior. The home looks brand new. "I'm Sharon. Please make yourselves at home."

"Thanks, Sharon. I'm Abel. This is my girlfriend, Cara."

We both shake her hand. "Please feel free to look around and let me know if you need anything."

I rest my hand on Cara's back and lead her through the house. The main level is open; it's one big great room, all with dark wood floors and neutral colors on the walls. The kitchen cabinets are dark, with a lighter granite countertop, and black appliances. We both step out back onto the expansive deck that tops more plush, green grass. "Abel, this is beautiful. But I'm sure this neighborhood is far above our price range."

"Babe, we don't even have a price range. Do you have any idea how much my loft is?" She shakes her head. "It's a lot, and when I work summer shifts fighting wildfires, I make enough to pay for a whole year's worth of payments. You don't pay any rent right now and you don't have a car payment, so I think we can afford to live here."

"Could you imagine? It's beautiful."

"I could definitely imagine. Let's keep looking around," I say.

We head inside to look at the rest of the house. There are four bedrooms, four bathrooms, a media room, and a loft. Sharon meets us at the bottom of the stairs as we come down. "So what do you think?"

"We love it," Cara says.

"Wonderful! Have you been looking for a new home for long?"

We both look at each other, and I say, "Actually, this is our first."

"Should we make this your last?" Sharon asks.

"Maybe you could enlighten us, we were discussing our budget and what we can afford."

"That's the beauty of what I do. My agency handles everything. I take it that you don't have a realtor?"

"No, we don't."

"Let's get a contract in so you're first in line. Then you can go home and I'll e-mail you the link for the loan. You can apply there and we'll see about getting you pre-approved."

I look at Cara and she is gnawing on her bottom lip. "What do you think, baby?"

She nods her head and we take the next thirty minutes going over all of the details and as we leave, we walk out with Sharon and she switches the sign on the house from 'open' to 'under contract.'

She waves and heads back inside. We sit and watch all of the lights being turned off. "Abel, did that really just happen?"

Leaning over the armrest, I grab her cheek. "Yes, baby, it did. I promised to take care of you and the baby forever. I want to give you both a forever home. It felt right, so I went with it. All I want to do is make you happy."

"You do make me happy. You have no idea. I mean, you just bought me a fucking house!"

"No, *we* just bought a house."

As we pull away from what I can only hope will be

our new home, I look over at Cara and she has a colossal grin on her face. There's a twinkle in her eyes and I wonder what the thoughts are that swirl in her mind.

"Baby," she says.

"Yeah?" I respond back squeezing her hand a little tighter.

"Can we not tell anyone about the house until all of the details are worked out?"

"Sure, but why not?"

"Since Bridgette's moving in today, I want it to be special for her. I don't want to take that away or trump her day by sharing our news. Plus, this is far from done. We need to work out all of the details of the loan and make sure our contract is accepted."

"Whatever you want to do is fine with me."

"Thanks," she says and drifts back off, gazing out the passenger window.

Pulling up to her condo, everyone is there, and I watch as Troy backs the U-Haul into the driveway. "Shit, does she really have that much stuff?" I ask.

Cara shrugs her shoulders as we get out of the car together. "Hey, guys," she says hugging Alexa.

"Why's Troy backing the U-Haul up?" I ask Bridgette.

"He said, and I quote, 'You're too small to be driving that thing.'"

I can't help but laugh. "Yup, that sounds like Troy."

Troy gets out of the truck and comes over to us.

"What's up, man?" I say, giving him a hug. "Thanks for helping out"

"No problem. Should we start unloading?" he asks.

Bridgette blushes a bit and says, "Yeah, of course."

The girls giggle, and Vince and I just look at each other. Hopefully this isn't going to take all day. Troy walks off first and opens the back of the U-Haul. He climbs in and reaches for Bridgette's hand. She takes it and hops in the truck with him.

Walking up, I pull the ramp out and they look at me. "There's a ramp here we can use; that's probably easier."

They each grab a box and walk down it. Cara starts to walk into the truck with Alexa and I stop her. "No way, kitten, you're not lifting a thing. You can unpack, but otherwise I'm putting my foot down." She glares at me and I lift her off of the ramp and set her on her own two feet. "In you go."

"God, you are so controlling," she yells back as she saunters into the house.

Alexa walks in with her. "They are obviously cut from the same cloth; Vince is the same way."

Watching the two of them walk off, I can't help but get excited that soon enough, Cara and I will be moving into our home. My mind whirls with thoughts of sleepless nights from not only endless hours of love making, but from the sweet cries of our newborn child. I envision Cara singing to our baby in the room we picked out to be a nursery, her blonde hair in front of her face while her delicate hand caresses the baby's cheek.

I don't know how or why I got so lucky but I did; my determination really paid off. One of the things my mom taught me was to never give up. I only hope to be half of the parent she was and to share those same lessons with our child.

ESSENTIALISM

a Life. Destiny. Fate. *novel*

The story of Bridgette and Troy

LK COLLINS

coming soon

Acknowledgements

To have completed this novel is yet again another dream come true. First, I have to thank my support system. My husband, you are my constant throughout all of this. You support me, drive me, and encourage me. I love your ideas and willingness to help. Thank you for being my rock. I love you to infinity and beyond, baby.

To my forever friend, Miranda, this one is for you. I don't think there are enough words to express the gratitude I have for you. The countless number of hours you spent helping me mold this baby are too many to count. I love when you believe in something, you tell me over and over again — that's a true friend. Your honesty is one of your best qualities and one of the many things I love about you.

To my wonderful editor, Lisa Christman of Adept Edits, what can I say about you that could sum up this experience? I truly have no words, except for how mind-blowing you are at what you do. Working with you was like nothing I've ever experienced. You made this process the best. Thank you for the countless hours of work, anal retentiveness, and most importantly honesty. You might have diagnosed me with a repetition disorder, but in doing so you've made me a better writer. From the bottom of my heart, I'm indebted to you always and am extremely grateful for everything.

To the best group of beta readers a girl could ask for. Kate, you are my best friend and my number one, but you know that. These books would *not* be the perfection they are without you. JC Emery, thank you for helping me to become a better writer and shaping this story. RL Griffin, as always your help means the world to me. I love working with you and can't thank you enough for your honest feedback. Christina, bringing you on board has been one of my best decisions. You're an amazing beta reader and I'm excited to work with you for the rest of the series — and then some. You have a true talent when it comes to beta reading and I'm claiming you. Colleen, you have a keen sense for detail and I love that you caught all of the little things. Thank you for making sure my medical terminology was up to par. Louise, thanks for the kudos — touch wood, girl!

For two special ladies whom I can't thank enough, I appreciate your hard work, drive for perfection, and quick turnaround time on this baby. Natasha, I was blown away by your expertise and am so grateful for your help. Leticia, you, my darling, are a gem. I don't know how I got so lucky to find you, but I did. Thank you both for everything.

For my media team, your countless hours of help made this book a reality. Allie Brennan of B Design, thank you yet again for creating another flawless and beautiful cover. Danielle Torella, you never cease to amaze me — Determinism's trailer is a *true* masterpiece and literally took my breath away. You brought tears to my eyes and in a good way. I appreciate your willingness to tackle yet another project.

And last but certainly not least, my fellow authors, readers, and bloggers. Your support throughout this journey has touched my heart in a way I cannot put into words. I never knew there were so many amazing people out there that would fall in love with my characters like I have. I've learned so much from each and every one of you. Thank you from the bottom of my heart and my characters'.

Love, LK.

XOXO.

www.ingramcontent.com/pod-product-compliance
Lightning Source LLC
Chambersburg PA
CBHW022141170626
46807CB00005B/2030